A Biological Storm

A Dora Ellison Mystery

Book 4

A Biological Storm
A Dora Ellison Mystery
Book 4

First Edition

By David E. Feldman

For George Ramos—a dear friend

TABLE OF CONTENTS

Prologue

The woman was exhausted. It had been a long day, beginning with her watch's alarm tapping her wrist to wake her up, then a walk with Charmer, her dark brown labradoodle, followed immediately by his breakfast, and then hers. Only then had she been able to change from her pajamas to the colorful clothes she would wear for the day.

She'd then put in a full shift at the salon; Shelly was a colorist, and she loved her job. She met men and women of all backgrounds, races, religions—all walks of life. She had gotten to know many of her clients, many of whom insisted that she, and no one else, color their hair. She had come to know most of her clients well. They trusted her with their hair and often with their secrets. She knew them. She loved them.

Today had begun like so many other days, listening to the joys and sorrows of her clients while she beautified and satisfied. Her work was challenging and often exhausting—today particularly so, because she had taken a last-minute client that had kept her late at the salon, and by the time she left, it was nearly eleven, an hour and a half past closing, and as far as she could tell, she was the only one left in the shop. She put away her products and equipment, cleaned up, closed up, locked up, and exited the rear of the shop into the parking lot, where she had parked her car that morning.

She never reached her car. A voice stopped her. Someone was calling her name. She turned and saw a small figure off to one side. Then headlights froze her in their glare; a vehicle's door opened. She shielded her eyes with a palm and squinted into the light. For some reason, her mind wandered to her dog, Charmer. A question formed on her lips, but an instant later the center of her body was torn to shreds, accompanied by a sound like a half-dozen deep-throated firecrackers going off almost simultaneously.

The question died on her lips.

Chapter 1

Dora was sitting at one of the two desks in the back of the storefront that was the office of Geller Investigations. Adam Geller sat at the other desk, turned toward the back of the room, leaning back in his office chair and watching a rerun of *The Odd Couple* TV show, his personal favorite, on his iPad.

Dora was reading a newspaper on her computer and shaking her head.

"This congressman is a real piece of work," she commented. "Multiple female assistants of his accuse him of inappropriate sexual behavior at work, and he doubles down—says it can't be true because none of them are up to his standards." She looked up from the paper at Adam, but the owner of Geller Investigations had finally put down his device and begun scrolling through photos he had taken the previous evening of a new client's soon-to-be ex-husband, who was dining at an out-of-town restaurant with a woman half his age. The couple was sitting next to, rather than across from, one another and leaning close, whispering into one another's ears and occasionally kissing.

"It's been like that since caveman times," blared the foghorn alto from the front of the office. "Today's women don't know how to use their assets."

"Really?" Dora answered. "What if they don't want to? What if the advances are unwelcome? Do you have any idea of how often women have to deal with crass, smelly, ugly bosses or co-workers? Don't they get to live and work in peace, if that's what they want?"

Thelma, the aging office manager with the foghorn voice, appeared in the doorway between the front and back of the office and leaned against the door jamb with her shoulder. "Gotta deal with reality," she observed. "What do you suggest they do about it?"

Dora lifted one of her feet a short way into the air. "Steel-toed boots."

Thelma chuckled and went back to work just as the chimes on the front door jangled.

"My name is Sawyer Townsend," said a low, husky voice in a timbre that made Dora look up and pay attention, though she couldn't see the voice's owner from the back room. "And I'm here about a missing person."

"Have you been to the police?" Thelma asked, her tone suggesting that she had not yet looked up from the invoices she was typing.

"I don't want the police involved," the prospective client answered.

"Why's that?" Thelma continued.

"Because I said so."

Dora smiled. Thelma was not used to being spoken to so firmly.

"You'll want our new client investigator," Thelma answered after barely a beat. "Dora Ellison. She's in the back, with the owner."

"Why wouldn't I want the owner?"

After a beat of silence, Sawyer Townsend appeared in the doorway. She was tall, perhaps five foot ten, slender, and about thirty years old.

She was dressed in a two-piece track suit—a glittering gold top with a black racing stripe running the length of each arm and a black spandex bottom with sparkling gold stripes on the outside of each leg. Her make-up was subtle and attractive and accented her bronze skin. Her hair was black with golden highlights.

Townsend's eyes traveled over Adam and reached Dora; she smiled faintly.

Dora stood. "C'mon in. I'm Dora Ellison." Dora was five feet eight inches tall and one hundred fifty-five pounds of muscle; she trained three days a week at Shay's Mixed Martial Arts. She walked lightly, on the balls of her feet, like the athlete she was. Her dark brown hair was medium length, and her skin was a pale beige. She held out a fist, and Townsend looked briefly at it before realizing the intent behind it. She did an awkward fist bump.

"My name is Sawyer Townsend," the woman began.

"So I heard," Dora said, and the woman looked befuddled, so Dora nodded in the direction of the outer office. "Just now."

"Ohh." Townsend laughed a little; her smile brightened slightly. "I'm the owner of—"

"Why don't you sit down?" Dora indicated a nearby chair, then fetched it and placed it beside her desk. Townsend sat.

"Thank you."

"You were saying?"

"Right. I'm the owner of the Rainbow Salon, two blocks west of here."

"Oh, yes. I've heard good things."

Townsend smiled again. "Thank you."

"How long have you been here?"

"Just a few moments; I came in—" She nodded toward the outer office, then blushed, realizing her *faux pas.* "We've been here about six months—five, actually. Well, five and a half. My situation has me a little distracted," she said apologetically.

"Would you like some coffee?" Dora asked, hoping to put the nervous young woman at ease.

"Actually, I've got to get back. Thought maybe I could—we could get the ball rolling with whatever you need."

"Okay," Dora agreed. "Let's start with what *you* need. We can always pick up where you left off—especially given that we're practically neighbors."

Townsend nodded and swallowed. "I'm here about my colorist. Her name is Shelly. Shelly Borzer."

"And she's missing?"

Townsend looked stunned. "How—how did you know?"

"Didn't you mention it to Thelma when you came in?"

"Thelma?"

The poor woman looked so confused that Dora briefly wondered if she were high or drunk, then decided she was not. But she was terribly stressed and possibly grief-stricken.

"Let's start with you telling me about Shelly." Dora caught Townsend's eye with a look that seemed to steady the woman, who took a breath, and began to explain.

"As you know, we're the new guys in town. Shelly used to work at Cut 'N Shape, one of our competitors—the ritzy, pinky-finger-in-the-air place that positions themselves as a spa." She scoffed. "They really do think they're a spa!" Sawyer touched her thumb to her forefinger, made a little circle, extended a pinkie and waved her hand in the air. "There's also another place called Time to Shine, but they specialize in people of color. At my place, Rainbow, we want to serve everybody. I mean, why not? We have people who know how to cut and color any sort of hair, and well—getting back to Shelly, everyone loved her. She just knew, I mean intuitively knew, what you needed and what you'd love. People intuitively knew they could trust her—confide in her. And they did. And she was always, always right. She was sort of"—she groped for the word —"a hair savant." She dug into a pants pocket, retrieved a phone, and began scrolling through photos. "Here she is." She held out the phone to Dora, who saw a photo, obviously taken at the salon, of a lean, fair-skinned woman with a clean complexion and amber hair in a jazzed-up pixie cut. Her smile was so warm and welcoming that Dora instinctively wanted to get to know her.

"How long has she been missing?" Dora asked.

"Since yesterday. She had a late appointment she had to take care of. She never came in today and never called. Shelly would never do that. I went to her house and knocked. I called a bunch of times. Nothing."

Dora thought about this. "What can you tell me about the late appointment?"

"Nona Cavaletti. Ninety-four years old. She hardly sleeps, so her appointments are always the last of the day."

Dora nodded. "Does someone drive her here?"

Townsend smiled. "Believe it or not, she uses Lyft. Little old lady with her app."

Dora concentrated, her features tightened, her expression pensive. "I'm assuming there was nothing notable about that appointment as far as you know."

Townsend shook her head. "It's logged in and out of our appointment book, as all appointments have to be."

Dora nodded. "Have you filed a police report?"

"Not yet," Townsend answered. "I suppose I should."

"The police are professionals."

Townsend sighed worriedly. "Well, I'm concerned about publicity—the wrong kind."

"My friend, Charlie Bernelli, who owns an ad agency here in town, says all publicity is good for business."

Townsend equivocated. "Not sure I agree. I'm…careful with my business."

Dora raised her eyebrows. Townsend looked away and gave a little shrug. Dora wondered if the woman's shyness derived from the pain and confusion of her missing employee or something else. Most salon owners she had known, and she had known many, were effusive natural marketers—steeped in the banter, intimacy, and garrulous gossip that was so often foundational to the salon experience. Of course, the flavor of every salon's ambience was unique, often an extension of its owner's, hairdressers', or colorists' personalities.

As if reading her mind, Townsend turned back to Dora and fixed her with a warm smile—a smile Dora found slightly disconcerting, and she had to think about why that was. People rarely made her uncomfortable, and she could not place what it was about Sawyer that was somehow just a little bit off.

"Well, we don't want any bad publicity. Besides, Rainbow's personality flowed from Shelly—everybody loved Shelly! I said that, didn't I? Well, it's important. She was everyone's best friend. Really!" Sawyer touched the tips of her fingers to her lips, then kept her hand in front of her face, waving her palm this way and that, fanning herself as she emphasized her words. "You trusted Shelly as soon as you met her. Everybody did. She was effervescent, filled with joy. And she knew exactly the right color or combo of colors for everyone. It was a gift!" Sawyer's fingers went again to her mouth. "Oh, my God. I'm talking about her in the past tense!" Her eyes filled with tears and her palm again waved to and fro, fanning her face. "Everybody, just everybody loved Shelly!"

Dora pressed her lips together, thinking, *Perhaps...perhaps not.*

• • •

After picking Missy up at the library, Dora drove to the Beach City Medical Center, where they pulled into a spot not far from the main building. While people were entering or exiting the lot or walking between their cars and the hospital's main entrance, today's activity seemed sedate compared with the recent tumult surrounding the formation of the hospital workers' union and the spate of medical murders at the hospital that Dora and Missy had helped to solve.

As the two investigators walked toward the building, they passed a petite, voluptuous, dark-skinned woman with short, sienna hair, wearing a crimson sweater, blue jeans, and brown boots. She faced a tall, pale man with dirty blond hair, dressed in a green medical employee's shirt, complete with name tag and job description, along with the BCMC logo.

"Look, I'm tired. I just don't want to go to your place. It's been a long day, and I've been dealing with really difficult people at more than one insurance company."

The man waved a hand, dismissing her reasoning. "You can rest at my place, Marsha. We'll pick up dinner, and you can chill to your heart's content."

The woman shook her head. "I know what you have in mind, and it isn't chilling. Not today, Brad. Okay?"

Brad's hand, which had waved in Marsha's direction, descended, and he grabbed her wrist between his thumb and forefinger.

Instantly, Dora slowed; Missy followed suit. *Uh, oh,* Missy thought.

"I just don't want to go to your place today is all," Marsha insisted. "What's the big deal?"

"There's no big deal," Brad replied. "It's just that you do want to come. You do—your brain just hasn't figured it out yet."

Dora glanced at Missy who, she could see, knew what was coming.

"I ought to know what I want." Marsha tried to wrench her arm away, but Brad was too strong.

"I agree!" Brad exclaimed. "But you don't. You should, but you don't."

Marsha sighed and stopped trying to pull away. "Listen, let's talk about it tomorrow at work. Let's take it slow. I like you, Brad."

"I know you do, Marsha. And you know you do, only you don't know how much. Come on." He began dragging her toward a nearby red Chevy pickup. "We'll go to my place and talk about it there. It'll be fine. You'll be glad you did. Promise!"

Marsha had relaxed the tension in her arm, but now used all her weight to hurl herself away from Brad, and she succeeded in breaking free and taking several steps away from his truck. But Brad was fast; he lurched in her direction, snaking his arm toward her wrist, his fingers grasping for purchase.

As fast as Brad was, Dora was faster. Despite her size, she was as light on her feet as any dancer. She was not a dancer, however; she was a high-level, amateur martial artist—an MMA competitor who preferred the no-rules version of street fighting to anything one saw in a gym or an octagon.

"Easy, Brad," Dora urged, gripping his wrist much as he had gripped Marsha's, though in a far more technically sound jiu jitsu hold designed to allow her access to any of his fingers, should she decide to slide her grip in their direction, or to allow her to bend the hand back, breaking the wrist, if she so desired. So far, she had no such desire, but she was waiting to see what happened next.

What happened was what usually happened in these street encounters: Missy groaned, concerned that they might end up in a police station with some unfortunately incomplete video from someone's phone as evidence. Brad struggled to pull free, as most men did, causing Dora to apply pressure, in this case to Brad's thumb. Brad screamed and instantly sank to his knees.

"You need to accept what Marsha is saying, Brad. She's not coming to your place today." Dora turned to Marsha. "I suggest, Marsha, that you refrain from going with him any other day, too—though of course, you're free to do whatever you like. The guy's bad news. And anyway, you can do so much better."

"Who the fuck are you?" Brad whined, looking wildly around. "This lady's attacking me! Does anybody see this? Can anybody take some video?"

"You sure you want people seeing your big man self—what are you, six two?"

"Six three," Brad moaned, reflexively.

"You want people seeing me kicking your ass all over social media? Why not just leave the lady alone, let her go on her way, and I'll let you be on yours?"

Brad didn't answer, but he also didn't move, and Dora watched as Marsha walked away.

She smiled at Brad. "Good choice."

Chapter 2

Neither Dora nor Missy spoke as they walked the short distance to the hospital entrance. As they approached and the automatic doors swooshed open, Dora pulled Missy aside.

"I'm sorry, Miss. I know you hate when I do that."

Missy had tears in her eyes; blinking, she wiped them away with the forefingers of either hand. "One day, someone'll have a gun, and that'll be the end of you—and of us." Missy was not much more than five feet tall, and she was rounder and softer than Dora, with features that spoke of her South Asian heritage. While Dora's favorite past times were violent mixed martial arts and street fighting, Missy's was curling up with a good book. Both women loved puzzles. Dora loved traditional puzzles—images cut into pieces—while Missy loved Sudoku, which were puzzles comprised of numbers—in rows, columns and squares. Their mutual love of puzzles led them to join together at Geller Investigations to solve crimes—a different sort of puzzle.

Dora sighed. "I know. You're right. But do you have any idea how much sexual innuendo and just plain abuse most women take?"

"What am I, a guy? Of course I do. It's disgusting. I took it from kids when I was in grade school, teachers and teacher's aides in high school, professors and other students in college, and co-workers, bosses, and goodness, people on the street as a grown up. I get it. Men think they can say stuff 'cause they figure you're weaker—"

"Or," Dora mused, "they think it's what you want. Well it *is* abuse, and it's about time someone stood up to some of these jackasses." She grinned.

But Missy did not return her smile. "So you're the sexual abuse police, now?"

Dora shielded her eyes with the palm of her left hand. She shook her head. "I apologize if you feel I put you in danger, but I promise—" She looked Missy in the eye, and when Missy looked away, she took Missy's chin between her thumb and forefingers and turned her face back, so that they were again looking at one another. "I promise—I am here to protect you, not the opposite. Always."

Missy pressed her lips together and nodded, her eyes tearing.

"Listen," Dora continued, "I've been thinking about something. What do you say we move in together?"

"What?" Missy was startled. Frustrated, she wiped her tears away. "Let's go in. We can talk about that later. People're looking at us through the window."

As the automated doors parted and they entered the hospital lobby, Charlie Bernelli rushed from the window, where he and his wife, Christine Pearsall-Bernelli, who was also Beach City's mayor, had been watching them. Charlie's face was a mask of intensity—part excitement, part exhaustion, part terror; he began accosting the two investigators with long, barely punctuated sentences.

"Sarah's been in labor for five and a half hours and C3's been with her the whole time—betcha she's doing better than he is—ha! Just kidding. I sure hope she's got good meds or an epidural or something—I mean, how long can the kid take to come out, you know? I wonder how it is for him in there, and I hope they've changed doctors at some point —I mean she loves her doctor, but can they maintain focus for whole shifts? I'm guessing they have nurses in there with them—at least one nurse, probably more, what do you think?" He gesticulated as he spoke, punching and poking the air, his long gray-blond hair whirling about his head. He smelled of a combination of his usual cologne and fear-driven sweat.

Dora didn't answer but watched him, wondering if he was on some kind of drug or if he was merely wired from exhaustion and stress over the birth of his granddaughter.

Charlie looked back at her, then at Missy, then back at Dora. "What? Do I have food between my teeth?" He began picking at his teeth with a thumbnail.

Dora enveloped him in a bear hug. "Charlie, Charlie, Charlie." She shook her head.

He grinned and waved at Missy, who waved back.

They headed as a group back toward the little cluster of chairs near the window, where Christine was still seated. She stood up, beaming, as they approached.

"Grandma!" Dora exclaimed, pulling Christine into another of her bear hugs.

Christine pulled back and gave Dora a dirty look, at which Dora burst out laughing. She noticed that Christine's reddish-brown hair was in a new, layered style and was now streaked with gray. Otherwise, the mayor looked as she usually did—fit, cheerful, and smart-looking in a navy blue business suit that was as conservative as her socio-political outlook. Christine smiled warmly at Missy, who held up a hand.

"No hugging for me," Missy said apologetically. "I'm still COVID-cautious."

Charlie had pulled two more chairs over from a nearby table, and they all sat down.

"I like the new hair," Dora said to Christine.

Christine shrugged ruefully. "Really? My usual colorist wasn't in the last time at Rainbow, and the roots had already begun to grow out. Meanwhile, I went to another shop, Cut 'N Shape, to cut my hair. Actually, I don't love it. I'll have Shelly color it next time."

"I love it both ways," Dora answered diplomatically. "But somehow, the usual way is more 'you,' though it could be I'm just used to that."

"Well, I hope she's back soon," Christine sighed.

Dora looked at Charlie, who had not sat down but was pacing in circles around the group.

"Stop," Dora protested, squinting. "You're making me dizzy. Anyway, how's work?"

Charlie sat down and leaned toward Dora, still babbling. "Fantastic! New client—HelthE Snax—owner Dean Clayburgh…bit of a…all about his cars, boats, houses…measures his dick by his…lots of work though…love it." Before Dora could answer, he was up again and pacing in the opposite direction. He seemed to be leaving out parts of his sentences, as though his brain were moving so fast it could not stop for every word.

C3 came through a door at the far end of the lobby, wearing hospital greens and a broad smile. "Olivia is here! Six pounds, four ounces! Sixteen inches!"

Charlie rushed over to him. "Is she…?"

"Don't start with me, Dad. She's breathing. She's crying. Your granddaughter is here!"

Charlie was a little crestfallen and more than a little annoyed but hid both well. "How's Sarah?"

"Exhausted. She's dozing right now, with Olivia in her arms."

Christine had encircled one of her arms through one of Charlie's, and her other arm had gone round C3's shoulder. For just a moment, they looked like any other happily growing family.

• • •

Prior to the salon's opening the next day, Dora met again with Sawyer Townsend, this time in Sawyer's office at the Rainbow Salon which, except for the office, was made up of a single wide, mirrored room with swiveling chairs along both sides. Missy, meanwhile, interviewed stylists and colorists in the waiting area in the front, which was two small couches that faced one another, along with several plush armchairs. The furniture and walls were chocolate-colored with bright rainbow swirling shapes painted in a style that, to Dora, evoked the psychedelic sensibilities of the 1960s. Tall posters in thin silver frames adorned the walls. The posters were prints of fashion photos of models of all ages—most of them women—sporting a variety of hair styles and colors.

Townsend's office matched the colorful style of the rest of the salon, but the photos on her walls were of a black Labrador retriever.

"Yours?" Dora asked.

Townsend nodded and smiled. "Lorelei," she said. "The love of my life."

"I have a Rottweiler-Doberman mix—a girl named Freedom."

"What a wonderful name!"

Dora grinned. "She's a rescue. Do you have family?"

Townsend nodded again toward the photos of Lorelei. "I'm out of touch with the human ones." Her hand went to her throat.

Dora nodded. "What can you tell me about Shelly's after work plans?"

Townsend's mouth twisted as she thought about the question. Then she shrugged. "Shelly was…is…a really private person. I'm trying to remember if she mentioned any plans, but I don't think she did. She never does. As far as I know, and I'm pretty sure that as far as anyone around her knows, Shelly's job is her life. She's just—" The salon owner searched for a word. "—effervescent. People trust her with their secrets. She's the sort of person you just intuitively know you can trust. And everyone does. She's our most popular colorist." Townsend's face fell. "We're sure to lose business unless she comes back."

"Does she have family?"

Townsend nodded. "Her parents are gone, but she has a brother—older."

"How old is Shelly?"

Townsend thought about the question, then shrugged. "I'm not sure, really. Mid-thirties, I'd say."

"Do you have any reason to believe she'd want to suddenly leave town?"

Townsend gave a firm shake of her head. "I not only don't—it's something Shelly wouldn't do without talking to me and making arrangements for her clients. She was…is so devoted to them. She loves them, and they love her."

"She has no significant other?"

Townsend shook her head again. "I…don't know."

Dora leaned forward, her elbows on her knees. "How competitive are the salons in town?"

Townsend took a deep breath and exhaled with a whoosh. "Well, we don't pay much overt attention to one another. I suppose the truth is we don't much like one another. There's gossip. We've heard things the other salon employees have said about us."

"Like what?"

"Like we water down some of our products. We charge too much…"

Dora nodded. "Business-related accusations."

"I'm not sure I'd say they rise—or fall—to the level of accusations." Townsend shrugged, and her lips tightened. "Just gossip. Nasty gossip, probably spread by jealous owners or ex-employees."

"Could any of them be jealous enough to do anything to Shelly?"

Townsend looked surprised. "Hurt her physically, you mean? I don't think so. I can't imagine anything like that. But stealing her away—luring her with money and promises. That's another thing."

Dora's eyebrows went up. "Do you think she'd go, for the right offer?"

Townsend didn't answer right away. "She loves it here. But for the right offer—who wouldn't?"

"So who might know more about her personal life?"

"Maybe one of the other stylists or colorists."

• • •

Missy, meanwhile, was already speaking with the salon's remaining colorist and two stylists. She sat with each of them individually, while Townsend shooed waiting customers to empty salon chairs so as to give them privacy.

Myra Levinson was a colorist who appeared to be in her late 40s, with deep reddish-purple hair whose color she referred to as "jam." She was friendly in a matronly, even motherly way. She wore a loose white blouse and a lavender peasant dress that gave her a hippyish vibe.

"I don't know much about Shelly's goings and comings on the last day she was here. We're all so close. I can't imagine why anyone might want to hurt Shelly."

Missy cocked her head to one side. "What do you think happened to her?"

Myra looked surprised. "I have no idea."

Missy frowned and nodded. "Isn't it possible she went off somewhere and for whatever reason didn't call in?"

"Of course it is." Myra nodded. "And I hope that's the case. But Shelly's always been so responsible. I can't imagine her not calling in." She laughed. "Unless she won the lottery or something. If I won the lottery, I wouldn't call anyone. I wouldn't want anyone to come begging at my door. I'd disappear, too. I'd change my phone number as well."

Missy made a mental note to ask Dora about Shelly's phone activity, assuming they could gain access.

Willa Spencer was a stylist who appeared to be barely out of her teens and claimed to have been styling hair professionally since she was fourteen, when she began working on her friends' hair. Willa had luxurious long, straight blonde hair of the sort many young and not-so-young women coveted. She had a carefree personality, but not with a hippy vibe. She was more of a cheerful, polite, nice-looking young woman with a ready smile and a positive word for and about everyone. She had not been aware that Shelly had a late client or that she'd closed the shop on the last day she'd been seen. Willa hadn't worked on that day.

She claimed to look up to Shelly as a role model—Shelly encouraged her to do whatever she wanted in life. To follow her dreams. She said she wished her mother was more like Shelly. After a moment, she said that Shelly was a kind of surrogate mother to her.

Estelle Robinson was a stylist who worked on most of Rainbow's Black clients. She was tall and lithe, with angular features. Her ebony cheekbones and chin were sharp, and she wore her hair in a short Afro with no makeup except for pink lipstick. A gold ring pierced one nostril, another the opposite ear. She was particularly skilled in pixie cuts, corn rows of just about any thickness, box braids, dreadlocks, hair twists, long and short cuts, blunt cuts, loose waves that used hair oil to tame the frizz, curly bobs, updos, slicked back bobs, Afros, faux hawks, buzz cuts, high ponytails, low buns, and high crown braids.

When asked about Shelly, she shrugged, and her eyes went cold, and Missy wondered if this were because she didn't want to talk about Shelly or because she didn't want to talk to her and Missy at all. So Missy asked if Estelle got along with Shelly. She got along with Shelly "just fine," Estelle claimed. She got along with everybody, but her demeanor said that she didn't have to like it.

Missy found Townsend's office, where Dora was just finishing interviewing the salon owner, and together they made their way out of the salon and to Dora's turbo. Their next stops were the two other salons in Beach City. Dora had started the car and was about to pull away, when Willa Spencer hurried out the salon door and toward the car, waving. Dora rolled down the window.

"I'm glad I caught you," Willa said as she lit a cigarette. "I said I was coming outside for a ciggy break, which is true." She waved the cigarette as evidence.

Dora waited, watching her. Willa shifted from one foot to the other.

"About Shelly's clients. She had a few weirdos. In fact, she was known for weirdo clients."

Dora narrowed her eyes. "Weirdos?"

"Just…weirdos." Willa shrugged and looked into the distance. "People—women who were hiding things."

Dora digested this. "Hiding things?" She'd found that repeating clients last phrases often encouraged them to open up.

Willa's eyes widened. "You just knew. When they said hello, they were…secretive. They didn't mean 'hello,' they meant 'get away from me—I've got my own shit to deal with.'"

"Anyone could be like that," Missy ventured. "Anyone with stuff on their mind."

Willa's mouth twisted as she thought about this. "True, but…these women were different. If I were you, I'd talk to them."

"Okay," Dora agreed, taking out her phone to make a note of the names. "Who were they?"

Willa looked skyward, thinking, then began listing the names of some of Shelly Borzer's clients.

Chapter 3

Barb Skolnick was, according to Willa, one of Shelly Borzer's regular customers. She was also the owner of the BS Pool Hall which, Dora noted, was an interesting name for a potentially dicey business establishment.

Willa had thought that Skolnick was not so much worthy of suspicion of anything in particular, as she was of being associated with troublemakers in general, many of whom caroused noisily at night at and around her establishment. Some were known to be involved in fights and the local, smalltime drug trade.

Dora found Barb behind a counter that tripled as cash register, cue and balls dispenser and mini serving station for hot dogs, burgers, sodas, and beer. Dora's meeting with Skolnick was brief and to the point.

"Hi," Dora said, "I'm looking for Barb Skolnick."

"Well," said the hefty amber woman with long, dark, shaggy hair that was far too black to be her natural color, and who was clad entirely in blue denim, "you've found her."

"They tell me over at the Rainbow Salon that you get your hair done over there with Shelly Borzer."

Skolnick immediately grew suspicious. She looked at Dora more closely. "Why would you want to know that? While I think I look okay, I'm not too sure people are clamoring to know who does my hair."

Dora chuckled. "No, though you look just fine. Shelly Borzer's missing. I believe she was your colorist?"

Skolnick looked concerned and slightly stunned. "What?"

Now it was Dora who was looking closely at Skolnick.

"What do you mean, missing?" the woman asked.

Dora ignored the question. "When was the last time you saw her?"

Skolnick's eyes wandered as she considered the question. "My last appointment was a week ago Thursday, 1:00 p.m. I open at 4:00, and I like to have at least a half hour to an hour free before I get in. Thursday's the start of the weekend here. Fridays and Saturdays that salon is crazy busy. You don't think anything's happened to her, do you?"

Dora raised her eyebrows, as if surprised. "Why would you think that?"

"I don't know. I watch too much subscription TV. Mysteries and thrillers, mostly. 'S how my mind works. Seriously, that girl's my colorist and confidant. I don't know who I'd talk to if she weren't around!"

"I don't suppose you'd want to talk about what sort of information you've trusted her with…"

Skolnick threw back her head and laughed. "First of all, no, I wouldn't, and second of all, I didn't kill her because she knows where the bodies are buried!"

Dora resisted asking, sarcastically, "Then why did you kill her?" She would take Skolnick at her word—for now.

• • •

 A Biological Storm

Kim Lamonte was the wife of Slim Lamonte, who was known as "Slime" because he was so slippery, in terms of being in and out of trouble—he was said to slip right out of any trouble he might find his way into. *Greasy as bacon* was how he referred to himself.

Physically, he was hefty verging on obese, whereas Kim was tall and lean. Dora thought of the old nursery rhyme she'd heard from her mother. *Jack Sprat could eat no fat. His wife could eat no lean*—only this couple was the reverse. Before seeking Kim out, Dora had researched her on the Internet, where she learned that the pair had allegedly been involved in local auto theft and loan sharking, though the latter had been Slim's purview, with the help of other select nefarious characters. Kim's role in the loan sharking had been as bait of sorts. Slim had been arrested five times with zero convictions, which may have had more to do with the skill of his lawyers than to any cleverness on his part. Kim was known to frequent Nails Tavern, where Dora found her at a table in the back. She was seated across from another, older woman, whose dyed blonde hair had obviously not been truly blonde for decades, if it ever had been. Once Dora approached, the woman looked at Kim who, with a sideways jerk of her head, told her to leave her alone with Dora.

"Okay to sit?" Dora asked.

Kim looked back at Dora, expressionless. Her small blue eyes hid in a weathered face surrounded by long, straw-colored hair. "Free country."

Dora sat. "I was wondering what you could tell me about Shelly Borzer."

Kim's eyes strayed to Dora's hair, which was just beyond shoulder length and brown and probably in need of some work. "I won't deny you need a good hair person, but Shelly's a colorist. Thinking of going blonde? In any case, I don't think she's booking anyone right now."

Dora looked surprised. "Why's that?"

"She's not around."

"Why's that?" Dora repeated.

Kim's chin came up, and her face shifted slightly to one side as she sized Dora up. "Why do you care?"

"Well, like you said, I might need some help with my hair."

"You do at that." Kim shifted in her chair. "But why would you come to me to ask about her, anyway?"

Dora looked more directly at Kim, allowing her features to open, projecting welcome honesty. "I'm a private investigator, and Shelly seems to have gone missing. Some of her friends have asked me to locate her."

Kim laughed. "Ha, ha—private dick!" She looked at Dora with new interest. "Who's the client?"

"I'm not at liberty to say."

Kim shrugged. "Probably Sawyer Townsend. That's who stands to lose if something happened to Shelly."

"Why might something have happened to Shelly?"

"Well, she's missing—maybe she used the wrong shade of blonde for someone's highlights. Some of us get crazy about our hair color. You'd better get it right—I should know." Kim leaned forward, her forearms on the table. "Look, I have no knowledge of anything happening to Shelly. I like Shelly. She takes great care of me; she's a sweetheart. But people like her run into trouble more often than not. You know?"

"People like her?" Dora narrowed her eyes. "What do you mean?"

Kim snorted a derisive laugh. "You're the private dick—you figure it out."

$\bullet \bullet \bullet$

Dora called Shay's Mixed Martial Arts to find out when the next class was and whether it was a lesson or sparring session or a combo class, which was both. There was no answer. She knew she'd dialed right, because the number was stored in her phone. She googled Shay's, and they did seem to be open on Saturday afternoons at three—in other words, now. And yet, they seem to be closed.

She was already wearing sweats, so she began stretching and thought she might do some *kata*, karate forms, which were always great for concentration and honing one's technique.

Her phone rang—Missy.

"Hey, Miss. I was just going to go over to Shay's to train for a few hours before dinner, but for some reason, they seem to be closed."

"So…when you work out there, what do you do?" Missy wanted to know.

Dora was sitting on the floor, her left leg folded up against her body, her right out in front of her. She put the phone down, hit "speaker," grasped her right toes, and gently pulled, allowing her hamstring and back to gradually open with the stretch. "Well, we stretch, go over technique, and spar. Then we usually review. It really depends. Some classes are more, well, classes. Shay teaches technique, especially to newer students—but to everyone, really. We're all always learning, even Shay. She picks up new techniques, or maybe I do. Or someone else. And we show everyone, go over the technique, practice it, and work out how to defend against it."

"What were you going to do today?"

"Depends on who was there. Apparently nothing, because she's closed for whatever reason—maybe something personal. Small businesses are like that—run by real people and subject to real-life situations."

"Well, since you're not going, why don't you teach me, and we can work out?"

Dora started to laugh, then realized that Missy was serious. "You? You're a librarian."

Missy sounded indignant. "That's right, and a significant aspect of my job is research—research and learning. Then we become expert. So this"—she gave a sheepish giggle—"this would be research."

"Come on over."

Ten minutes later, Dora touched Missy gently on the upper arm. "Miss, I never would have thought…" Moments later, they were seated facing one another on Dora's living room rug. Her dog, Freedom, who was part Rottweiler, part Doberman, looked on, apparently bemused.

Dora showed Missy how to stretch her neck, legs, arms, back, and shoulders; Missy was aware of some of the stretches, as she had availed herself of free yoga classes every now and then when she was in college and more recently at her library.

Dora then showed Missy how to perform a side kick.

"Huh," Missy mused. "I'm sorta *your* side kick."

Dora shook her head. "Don't dissociate. Focus on what you're doing. You need to turn your leg, chamber it, then at the apex of the lift, bring it back to your body, then extend to kick, using your base leg, which you turn at the end of the kick, giving it that final drive."

"That final *kick*," Missy giggled.

"This is serious."

Missy pressed her lips together and gave a solemn nod. "I guess it kind of scares me, so I make jokes. Sorta why I wanted to learn."

"Because it scares you?"

Missy nodded.

Dora approved. "That's good."

She then showed Missy the difference between a side kick and a roundhouse.

"If you ever need to use this stuff, a roundhouse to the back of your opponent's knee, which is pretty easy to do, can pull her leg out from under her. Then she's ripe for getting punched in the face with your opposite fist."

"I'm pretty sure I can manage that." Missy tried the roundhouse, which was awkward at best, then aimed a punch at Dora's face.

"Here's the thing," Dora said. "You're punching with your arm. You need to punch with your leg."

"What does that mean? Wouldn't a punch with your leg be a kick?"

"It means, you do like a hitter in baseball—"

"I don't watch baseball."

"Here, plant your leg and sort of crouch, but—yeah, like that, but not so much of a crouch. That's it! Then you kind of jump off that back leg while you're throwing the punch, which is where the power comes from."

"Oh, boy," Missy gasped, winded. "I'm going to need to practice. But I will! I'm gonna get better at this."

Dora grinned. "Well, you won't get worse. Sorry, I was kidding."

"No! You're right!"

Dora positioned Missy to try again. "This is key—hit your target— the person you're punching, dead on the jaw, preferably the side of the jaw. You hit anyone there, they're going down."

Missy's eyes went wide. "Even you?"

Dora nodded. "Even me."

• • •

The blonde highlights in Jocelyn's perfectly shaped shoulder length hair were very much the right shade. Missy suspected that a lot of time and consideration had gone into her color selection. Jocelyn (apparently no last name) was the owner of Cut 'N Shape, Beach City's chic salon, according to Jocelyn. In fact, the venue billed itself as the "New York metro area's chic salon."

Jocelyn wore a tight pink body suit that accentuated her curves, along with gold bracelets studded with diamonds, and diamond stud earrings.

Missy got right to the point, explaining that Shelly Borzer was missing. In response, Jocelyn said nothing, but merely looked back at Missy. They stared at one another for a long moment.

"Do you have any feelings about Shelly going missing?"

"Feelings?" Jocelyn mused. "My feeling is no great loss, though I suspect she'll turn up at some point. She wasn't the most reliable person."

"What do you mean?" Missy asked.

Jocelyn's go-to expression was one of permanent disdain. "At Cut 'N Shape, we have no need to pay any attention to the work done at any other salons. We are leaders in our field in the New York metro area. People pay attention to *us*."

"Really?"

"Really. And why she'd want to work for Sawyer Townsend I have no idea. That woman is a failed businessperson."

Missy's eyebrows went up. "Why do you say that? They seem busy enough."

Jocelyn gave a carefree laugh. "No one's *ever* busy enough. You're not in business, so you don't know."

"True," Missy admitted.

• • •

Gloria Watson was the owner of Time to Shine. Her golden skin fairly glowed, as did her bright smile and perfect teeth; her hair was done in a tight Afro. She showed Missy into a brightly lit office, where she sat behind a desk that was bordered by small, shiny black flowerpots containing colorful, well-tended orchids. She noticed Missy admiring them.

"My babies," she said proudly. "How can I help you?"

"My name is Missy Winters and—"

"Oh, the librarian!" Watson looked delighted.

Missy smiled. "That's right."

"I'm a big reader," Watson exclaimed, her eyes widening happily. "I read everything from poetry to fiction to"—she waved a hand at the matted posters on the walls—"biographies." The posters were of Richard Wright, Toni Morrison, Maya Angelou, and James Baldwin.

"So I noticed." Missy looked impressed. "Literary giants!"

Watson beamed, then sobered. "But you're not here to talk about great authors—not that we can't!" She laughed, a wonderful, musical sound.

"I'm here to talk about Shelly Borzer." Missy waited but Watson gave no sign of having understood.

"The colorist at the Rainbow Salon?"

Watson nodded but beyond that did not react. "I don't really follow our colleagues."

Missy noted the use of the word "colleagues" rather than "competitors." She looked down at her hands, which were folded in her lap, then back at the salon owner. "Shelly's gone missing. I work for Geller Investigations. We've been hired to find out why and what happened to her."

Gloria wriggled in her seat. "Ooh, a real mystery." She then grew serious. "While I've never had the pleasure, I do hope the woman is safe."

Chapter 4

Missy was looking out of her living room window at the Beach City business district. Her building had once been a school and was centrally located in the city's busiest shopping area. She enjoyed watching the different people walk by or stop and chat or get in and out of their cars; she sometimes made a game of imagining their lives. She did this for a few minutes but became distracted by a pair of cardinals in a tree several yards outside and to the left of her window. The tree grew in a corner of her building, in the little strip of lawn facing the street. She became aware of the cardinals' chirping distinct from the traffic sounds, and she closed her eyes and enjoyed the little symphony they provided.

When she opened her eyes, she saw Dora pulling up in her red Subaru turbo, with Freedom's head poking out of a rear window. Grinning, Missy watched Dora get out of the car and go around to the passenger side to let Freedom out on her leash. Missy took Comfort's leash from the little wooden table she kept just inside the door. As usual, Comfort heard the leash jangle and came running, and together they made their way downstairs to greet their guests.

The dogs cavorted and frolicked with one another until and unless they spotted another dog, when they would strain against their leashes to meet or bark at the newcomer.

"I noticed that the two salons I visited carry hair products made by Julienne Inc.," Missy pointed out, referencing the local company that had been in the middle of several recent local controversies.

Dora nodded. "Yup. At Rainbow too. I had no idea they were into hair products."

"From what you've told me, they're into money products."

"I wonder if they are somehow involved in what happened to Shelly," Dora pondered.

"Why would you think so?" Missy asked.

"Because trouble follows them. The people who run the place and their friends all seem kind of skeevey."

Missy glanced at Dora. "I suspect that won't stand up in court."

Dora smirked back at her. "We're not in court."

"Are you thinking something specific?" Missy pulled slowly on Comfort's leash, reeling him in and away from a black Pekinese in which he had expressed interest.

Dora shrugged. "Maybe she resisted their sales pitch. I wouldn't put breaking the law, even violence past them."

"Do you really think Shelly's missing because she didn't want to buy hair products?"

"Well, when you put it like that… Still, I can talk to Sawyer about it. Wait, I have an idea." Dora took out her phone, scrolled to a number in her addresses and pressed the dial and speaker buttons. "Sawyer Townsend?"

"Dora. Hi! That was fast."

"Oh, well, I just have a couple of questions. Do you have Shelly's address? I think it makes sense to see what her neighbors know."

Once they had her address, Dora and Missy drove to Shelly's street, which was in a section of Beach City dominated by bars and restaurants. Shelly's home was one of the few single-story capes among enormous lifted, hurricane-hardy homes. Hers was a striking shade of violet, high-lighted by cheerfully bright yellow shutters.

"She must pay a fortune in flood insurance," Missy mused. Super-storm Sandy had flooded most of the single-story homes in Beach City, and flood insurance rates had spiked in the years since.

"I suspect it's a rental, but yeah—the owner probably does."

They knocked on the doors of the homes on either side of Shelly's. At the second, a tall, balding, slow-moving sixtyish man in an orange T-shirt, beige shorts, and a lifelong beach tan opened his door and stepped outside. He looked at Dora and Missy, then at the sky. "Think it'll rain? I was hoping to hit the beach."

Dora looked up. "Doesn't look like it."

"The way the weather is these days, the storms show up before you know it. What can I do for you?"

"We're looking for information about your neighbor over there," Dora pointed. "Shelly Borzer."

"She seems to have disappeared," Missy added, and noted Dora's disapproving frown.

The man nodded slowly and cleared his throat with a phlegmy rum-ble as he considered the question. "Haven't seen her in a few days," he said after a long pause.

"Do you know her well?" Missy asked.

Another long pause, followed by another rumble. "Not really, but she has—a reputation."

"How so?" Dora asked.

"She's an avid churchgoer—Roman Catholic. Some of the members of our church don't like her. We don't like fornicators."

Missy looked surprised. "So she's a…fornicator?"

"So they say."

The man spoke so slowly Dora shifted impatiently on her feet.

"But aren't everyone's parents fornicators? And what does that mean exactly, anyway?" Dora wanted to know.

The man shrugged.

"What did you say your name was?" Dora asked.

"Didn't." The man turned, ambled back into his house, and closed the door behind him.

Dora and Missy looked at one another.

"Let's take a ride over to city hall," Dora suggested.

Missy agreed.

• • •

Fifteen minutes later, they presented themselves to John, the fiftyish security guard with curly auburn hair and a kind face who worked at the front desk, just inside the revolving doors on the ground floor of City Hall.

"Dora Ellison and Missy Winters to see the mayor," Dora said.

"Hey Dora. Is she expecting you?" John wanted to know.

"No, but we'll take our chances."

John dialed an extension on his phone. "Dora Ellison and Missy Winters are here to see the mayor…. No, they don't."

His eyes flicked to Dora and Missy. He nodded.

"Go on up. Third floor."

"We know," said Dora.

The mayor's office took up all but a small portion of the floor, with the remainder being a much smaller office belonging to the deputy mayor. Dora and Missy stepped off the elevator, into a faux doorway that held a security scanner. They emptied their pockets into the little bowls provided, which were handed by a police officer on one side of the scanner to another on the other side. When prompted, the two women stepped one by one through the scanner and had their belongings returned to them. They then rounded the corner together into the enormous office belonging to Beach City Mayor Christine Pearsall.

Christine sat behind a desk that nearly filled the far end of the fifteen-foot-wide room. City, state, and federal flags stood behind her, as did a portrait of the US president and a painting done by a local artist of a beach scene at one of the city's many renowned beaches. Christine finished signing the documents in front of her, stood, and held her arms out for Dora, who hugged her. Christine then held out an elbow to Missy for the post-COVID elbow touch which, along with the fist bump, was nearly ubiquitous in local official circles.

The mayor motioned them to sit down on the couch or any of the plush chairs that were arranged around the long, stained wooden coffee table at the other end of the room. "To what do I owe the pleasure?"

Dora described their meeting with Shelly Borzer's neighbor.

Christine nodded and smiled. "Manfred Fassbender. I know him, and I knew Shelly. She colored my hair."

"Something you said a while back made me think you knew her."

"They both go to my church."

"What is this thing about 'fornicators'?" Missy asked, and explained about Fassbender's comments.

Christine thought for a moment. "The Bible—Corinthians—defines fornication as sexual immorality. There's a list of offenses in Galatians verse 5, chapter 19 which reads," she recited, "'The acts of the flesh are obvious: sexual immorality, impurity and debauchery; idolatry and witchcraft; hatred, discord, jealousy, fits of rage, selfish ambition, dissensions, factions and envy; drunkenness, orgies, and the like.' So technically, pretty much everyone's a fornicator." She smiled.

Missy was amazed. "How do you remember all that?"

Christine laughed. "Been hearing it all my life. I was raised to believe that sexuality itself is immoral."

"Do you believe that?" Dora asked.

"Of course not. I believe sexuality is God-given."

Dora looked from Christine to Missy and back again to Christine. "So what do you think Fassbender was referring to when he said Shelly was a fornicator?"

Christine shrugged. "Some people in the church—and not in the church—are pretty judgmental. Everyone who really knew Shelly loved her."

"We keep hearing that," Dora commented.

"Well, there was one other neighbor of hers…" Christine was remembering. "Behind her."

"What?" Dora asked.

"We had an issue come to small claims. Something about a tree on Shelly's property. I think she had a portion of it cut down, and it damaged a little shed in the neighbor's yard."

"But doesn't she rent?" Missy asked.

"I think so," Christine answered. "But she was the one who hired this vendor. From what I remember, the neighbor sued the vendor and Shelly both, and the neighbor lost. He was pretty angry."

"What was his name?" Dora asked. "The neighbor, I mean."

Christine picked up a phone receiver that was on the coffee table in front of her and dialed an extension. She spoke briefly, then listened and hung up. "Records is pulling the information. When you leave, take the elevator up to four and tell them I sent you and what you're there for."

After retrieving the name and address of the neighbor who had filed the complaint against Shelly Borzer, Dora and Missy headed back to Shelly's neighborhood, found the address, and knocked. This time, the door was answered by a short, stocky man with longish black hair that was parted on one side and whose bangs curled beneath one eyebrow. He stared at them, waiting. Dora said nothing.

"Well?" said the man.

"Are you Donny Schmidt?"

"Who's asking?" the man wanted to know.

Dora took out a card and held it out. The man leaned forward, squinted at the card, but made no move to take it. "What are you investigating?"

"You had an altercation with your neighbor"—Dora nodded toward Shelly's house—"Shelly Borzer—sometime back?"

"Long time ago. So?"

"So Mr. Schmidt, Shelly's missing."

The man's lip curled in a sneer; he had a perpetual glint in his eye, as though he was always on the verge of some prank or that he knew a secret about whomever he was speaking with. "Am I supposed to care? I hope she's dead."

"You hope Shelly Borzer's dead? Really?"

Now Schmidt stepped outside and directly into Dora's space, crowding her, perhaps hoping to intimidate her into taking a step backward. She did the opposite, stepping closer to him, until they were nearly nose to nose, with Dora several inches the taller of the two.

"No law against that, is there—hoping a person's dead?"

"If there were, I could probably be arrested right now. So no." She smiled, and her encroaching into his space forced Schmidt off balance, and he finally had to take a small step backward. Dora stepped further into his space, making sure to grind her boot heel onto his toe.

"All sorts of things are…technically legal," she said, and they glared at one another. Dora could see Schmidt struggle against the pain. He tried to take another step back but was pinned by Dora's heel.

"Tell you this. The only reason she won her case is she's in bed with the mayor."

"What do you mean by that?" Missy asked, and Donny Schmidt regarded Missy with a look so full of malice that she inadvertently stepped behind Dora.

"I mean women like that look out for each other."

"Women like what?" Missy asked innocently.

"Women who like each other. They might as well have their own, you know"—he moved a fist back and forth in front of his crotch —"equipment."

Dora smiled. "I can pretty much guarantee you that the mayor is not gay, though if she were, why would you care? Does that somehow threaten your"—she mimicked the motion he'd just made —"equipment?"

Schmidt huffed, scoffing. "Huh! She turn you down?"

Dora looked back at Schmidt for a long moment. "Losing that case is still eating at you." She shook her head. "I feel sorry for you." She turned away. "Come on, Missy. We're done here."

As they approached Dora's car, they heard Schmidt's voice call after them. "Yeah, I still hate her guts, and I still wish she was dead! So what?"

Chapter 5

The tall, lean man who strode into the police station was handsome in a magazine ad sort of way, his face devoid of any hint of fat and the rest of him the same. He had prominent cheekbones above hollows of the sort that were admired by booking agents and advertisers because they conformed to the standards set by fashion magazines and designers. The dimples that appeared below the hollows when he smiled would also have been sought after by the fashion industry, except that he wasn't smiling now.

Working the walk-in window was Lieutenant Gary "Re" Morse, the gatekeeper at the Beach City Police Department—a man who was able to quote every rule and regulation verbatim and often did. He was obsessive and compulsive and exactly the man Chief Stalwell needed to keep the walk-in public in their place.

"How can I help you?" Morse asked.

The man said, "I'm here to report a missing person. My brother."

Morse held up a finger and turned his head to look behind him. "Lieutenant Trask?"

A uniformed policewoman with short red-brown hair emerged from the bowels of the station. She gave Morse a questioning look.

"Possible 10-65," he said, and nodded toward their visitor.

"Follow me, sir," Trask said as she came around Morse's desk and opened the door that stood between the lobby and the station proper. Lieutenant Catherine Trask was in her late twenties, slim, athletic and all business. The man followed her to a desk, where she told him to sit down while she opened a file in her computer. She asked the man his name, address, phone number and email address, and then asked him to tell her about the missing person.

The man swallowed and looked away. "I haven't seen my brother in five years. He'd had a falling out with our father and left, under extremely strained circumstances."

"This was five years ago? He's been missing since then?"

The man turned back to Lieutenant Trask. "That's right."

Trask smiled encouragingly. "Why don't you tell me what you do know?"

The man swallowed and looked at his hands, which were fidgeting in his lap. "My brother and my father had a terrible argument—screaming and throwing things. Back then, I mean."

"About what?" asked Trask.

Berger shook his head. "They'd always been oil and water—arguing about everything. If one said the sun was shining, the other swore it was raining."

The lieutenant looked steadily at Berger, waiting, but he didn't elaborate. "Go on," she said.

"And he, my brother, just stormed out. My father died soon after. Heart attack. We thought the fight might have contributed—"

"We?"

"My mother and I. My mother is, was, Camille. That's why I'm here, actually. My mother died."

"And there was a criminal element—?"

"Oh, no. She'd been ill. Cancer—pancreatic."

"I'm sorry for your loss."

"At least she went quickly. Anyway, she left quite a lot of money."

"To you and your brother?"

The man nodded. "Exactly. My father had inherited three million from his in-laws—my grandmother's parents—and he'd always been a good businessman, a smart investor, and he turned it into three hundred million."

"Impressive," Trask marveled.

"Yes, well, that's to be split between my brother and me. Only my brother seems to have…disappeared."

Trask nodded, her fingers poised above the keyboard. "Your brother's name?"

"Steven Berger. I'm his older brother, Lorne Berger."

Trask retrieved a form from her desk, affixed it to a clipboard, and passed it to Berger along with a pen. "Please fill this all the particulars about your brother, to whatever degree you can."

● ● ●

Dora and Missy were on the floor of Dora's apartment, which was in its usual messy state. Dora's head was in Missy's lap, and their two dogs, Comfort and Freedom, were on the floor nearby. Freedom was looking around anxiously at every sudden sound outside, while Comfort was fast asleep. Chopin's "Piano Prelude in E Minor" played on the stereo, and Dora's eyes were filled with tears, as they did anytime she heard Chopin, whose music inevitably reminded her of her sweet Franny, her lover, who had been killed not so long ago, run down by "Cranky" Franky Patella. She loved Chopin, and while she did not love the pain the music evoked, she found the music cathartic—she was determined to remind herself of Franny and feel her loss.

Something occurred to her, and she took out her phone and pressed a number. "Sawyer?"

"Speaking."

"Dora Ellison."

"Have you learned anything?"

"We have, but nothing we can report yet. I do have a question. Does your salon carry Julienne's products?"

"We do. Why do you ask?"

"Do you deal with a rep there?"

"We do. His name is…Anderson."

"Jeremy Anderson?"

"No. Ken Anderson, I believe. I think his father might be Jeremy— guy who owns a local ad agency."

"We've met. Jeremy's agency handles Julienne, and I believe he's a part owner."

"What's this about?"

"Probably nothing. Is there anything…off about the salon's interaction with Julienne?"

"Off? In what way?"

"Do they pressure you to buy the products?"

"Well, they give us a coupon. I think Anderson, the rep, brings them by when they deliver the product. You sure there's nothing you need to tell me about them?"

"If there is, I'll let you know." Dora ended the call and looked up at Missy, who met her eyes.

"Do we need to go over to Julienne?"

"Let's see if anything more develops," Dora said. "My experience has been that anything involving that place is corrupt, criminal, or otherwise dicey."

"So maybe we take a ride there."

"No, thanks. Just thinking about going there puts me on the edge of a panic attack."

Missy was surprised; she had rarely known Dora to show fear, but she also remembered the extremely violent attack Dora had endured at the Julienne facility.

As if reading her mind, Dora added, "If we find a compelling reason to further investigate Julienne, we'll go. But not until."

• • •

Once Lorne Berger had filled out the form in the chair next to her desk, Lieutenant Catherine Trask typed in its contents, printed them out, and brought them over to two desks, the fronts of which had been pushed together. They were the desks of the BCPD's lead detectives, Paul Ganderson and Gerald Mallard, who were known, though rarely in their presence, as the Goose and the Gander. As Trask approached their desks, a small smile played at her lips, not quite breaking across her face.

"Missing person," she said, glancing at Ganderson while dropping the paper on Mallard's desk. Ganderson stared back at her. He was moving a toothpick around his mouth with his tongue, trying absent-mindedly to pick his teeth without having to touch the toothpick. He was somewhat obsessive compulsive and easily annoyed. Several years earlier, he and Catherine Trask had briefly been an item, and now Trask despised him; she thought him sexist, possibly misogynistic. Both were characterizations that had some truth to them. The greater truth was, she had liked Ganderson, and he had hurt her, and now the lieutenant did everything she could to get her former lover and superior officer's gander, so to speak. After watching Trask saunter back to her desk, Ganderson stood up. He was tall—six foot three—with thin, black hair that was nearly always slicked back with gel, since he hated when his hair was mussed, whether by the wind, a physical altercation, or anything else. His face was pockmarked by the remnants of a bout of acne. He was a stickler for rules, and the rules were the senior member of the detective team is given the case.

So Ganderson stood up, walked around the side of his desk to Mallard's, took the sheet of paper Trask had deposited there, went back to his desk, and sat down. He glanced at Mallard, who did not seem to notice before putting his feet up on his desk, leaning back in his chair and beginning to read.

Mallard grinned to himself. He enjoyed his partner's frustration and little parade and was delighted by Trask's incessant needling. As Ganderson leaned back, stretching his legs, Mallard leaned forward and checked the creases in his pant legs. He wore an Italian cashmere and silk blend, single-breasted tailored suit that had cost him just over $8400. The suit was nowhere near his most expensive piece of clothing, but as he did with each of his suits and jackets, he had this one dry cleaned each time he wore it. Though it was nearly three years old, he had worn this particular suit only once before today.

Paul Ganderson's suit was brown; all his suits were brown. He had three. He was considering buying a black or perhaps a blue suit but had yet to pull the trigger. He was extremely frugal and reluctant to spend money on a suit that was not specifically required. He never had any of his suits cleaned unless he was literally rolling around in the dirt while wearing them, which had happened only once, while breaking up a fight outside a local bar.

While Ganderson was tall and lean and cultivated a Clint Eastwood-style squint and faraway look, Mallard was just shy of six feet tall and chunky, with salt and pepper hair, a gray mustache, and a way of speaking that often grated on the listener, especially if that listener was Ganderson.

Each detective cultivated and emphasized his own particular attributes and the two often clashed but rarely with any serious consequences;

their relationship was not so different from that of many married couples.

After a moment, Ganderson stood up and walked about halfway to Lieutenant Trask's desk and spoke loud enough so that everyone in the police station's main room, known as "the bullpen," could hear.

"For anyone not familiar with regulations, when you hand out new cases, regulation says you start at the top. Just a little refresher." He turned, returned to his desk, sat down, put his feet up, leaned back, and resumed reading.

Trask smiled to herself.

Mallard looked at his partner. "Er ah, whatcha got there ah, Paulie?"

Detective Ganderson finished reading Trask's initial report and slid the paper across the desk to his partner. He waited until Mallard finished reading, then beckoned in the direction of Trask's desk. "C'mon back, Mr. Berger."

Once Lorne Berger had made his way to a chair that was midway and to one side of Ganderson's and Mallard's desks and told his story, Ganderson began to speak. "So you haven't seen, heard from, or spoken to your brother in five years. You've had no communication with him at all?"

"That's right."

"Er, ah…" Mallard waved a finger, as though an idea was just now occurring to him. "Why, if he's been missing all this time, has no one been looking for him until now? This is all about the money?"

Berger looked surprised. "Who says no one's been looking for him? When our father died, his second wife, Camille, looked. She just didn't find him."

"And you?"

Berger shrugged. "My brother's a big boy. If he doesn't want to stay in touch with his family, that's his prerogative."

"You sound a little pissed off," Mallard observed.

Berger flashed the detective an annoyed look. "His disappearance was painful for our mother. She loved our father, and when he died and one of his sons wasn't available…" His voice trailed off.

"It might be helpful," Ganderson said, "if we knew what the argument with your father was about, especially if it precipitated your brother's disappearance."

Berger paused. "It was about Steven's life choices. Dad didn't approve."

"What sort of life choices?" Ganderson continued.

Berger looked steadily at the rumpled detective. "My parents were old fashioned, and my brother was…not."

"What does that mean?"

Berger seemed to be about to speak when Mallard interrupted.

"Was the disagreement in any way about money?"

Ganderson glared at his partner, then turned to Berger, who was shaking his head.

"No, it was about the way my brother was living his life."

"Did he drink? Was he into drugs?" Mallard asked.

"He had a few beers now and then—maybe a glass of wine. Little if anything more. And no drugs."

Ganderson was looking hard at his partner, but his question was addressed to Berger. "What did your brother do for a living?"

"He worked at a bank. First National here in Beach City—first as a teller and eventually as branch manager. He made a good living, was well liked, did his job well, and would have gone on to be a vice president—or so he believed."

Ganderson looked away from Mallard and toward Berger. "Is there anyone you can put us in touch with that he'd been close to before he left? Friends? A significant other?"

Berger nodded, took out his phone, and began scrolling through contact information. "This was his best friend. I haven't spoken to him because our father let it be known that he was not welcome in our home, and I thought reaching out to him might not go well. I figured I'd leave that to you."

Ganderson wrote down the information. "Barry Hutchins. So, this was his number and address five years ago? Do you know if it's current?"

Berger slowly shook his head. "Sorry. I have no idea."

Chapter 6

Dora and Missy were in Dora's turbo on the way to Beach City Roman Catholic Church, often referred to by locals as BCRC.

"So besides her church, where else could we go to talk to people about Shelly?"

Missy bit her lower lip as she concentrated. "We've been to probably the best source of local information and gossip—the salon. After the church, let's go back and look at Adam's databases."

"Good idea. Hopefully the priest will know more." Dora paused. "Um, there's something I want to get back to. Remember a while back I asked about us moving in together?" As Dora was changing lanes to turn onto a side street, a black pickup cut them off and veered to the side street to make the same turn. "Hey!" Dora gunned the turbo and, with a burst of speed, swerved around the truck, cutting it off as she made the turn in front of him. The driver of the pickup blasted a long note on his horn and began to tailgate them.

"Oh, for goodness' sake!" Missy rolled her eyes. "Stop it, Dora."

Dora slowed the turbo to a crawl. The truck's driver screamed at them and turned onto a different street. Dora grinned.

"Someday, someone's going to have a gun."

"Well," Dora answered, "they might have to use it."

They drove the rest of the way in silence. As they parked, Missy shot Dora a bleak look. "Since we're at a church, maybe I'll say a prayer for your driving."

Dora huffed. "Better to pray for the other guy."

Beach City Catholic was a large brick building a block from the beach. Its main area, which was taller and wider than the rest, housed the sanctuary. The smaller area was home to the rectory.

Outside the rectory, they found a fit man in his late sixties, of medium height, with a full head of white hair, a reddish complexion, and an easy smile. He was planting colorful impatiens in a newly turned flower bed. He heard them approach, and stood up, slapping his hands together to wipe away the dirt. He held them up and looked apologetic. "Still dirty." He shrugged. "I don't shake hands so much anymore anyway." He beckoned them to follow him into the church.

Inside the rectory was a large office, its walls lined with filled bookshelves. Two desks sat on either side of the central area, one of which was staffed by a large gray-haired woman with bright blue eyes and a navy blue dress. She looked at the priest as they entered. When he saw her, he must have realized she was waiting for an introduction.

"Mrs. Hornfield, this is…"

"Dora Ellison and Missy Winters," Dora supplied. "Private investigators."

"How exciting!" Mrs. Hornfield eagerly exclaimed. "Has there been a murder?"

"Not that I'm aware of." The priest looked at Dora and Missy, remembering. "I'm Father Walter Engells, but please call me Father Walt."

Without waiting for an answer, he turned and led them to his office, a cozier, darkened room, also lined with filled bookshelves. Missy stopped to examine the tomes.

"Do you like to read?" the priest asked.

"I do," Missy said. "I'm a librarian—part time."

Father Walt indicated the books. "Commentaries on the gospels and other religious-related writings, along with my share of classics. I, too, love to read."

He sat down behind a modest wooden desk and bade them sit in the chairs opposite. "Now, how can I help?"

"We've been hired to locate Shelly Borzer. She seems to have gone missing, and we understand she's a member of your congregation."

"That she is, and extremely popular. I hope she's okay." He looked concerned, realizing the possible gravity of the situation.

"What can you tell us about her?" Dora asked.

"Not very much I'm afraid, other than her being popular. She has a natural gregariousness—loves people, I suspect. Enjoys engaging with others—and very supportive. She'd probably be a natural in the clergy."

"Does the church have female clergy?" Missy wondered aloud.

Father Walt did not seem to have heard the question. "Beyond that, I can't say very much."

"Do you know anything about her personal life?" Dora asked. "Anyone with whom she might be…especially friendly?"

Father Walt looked down, then back up at the women. "Again, I can't say much about her personal life. Any conversations we might have had would be private, of course."

"Of course," Dora agreed. "But what about people she was friendly with at services? Surely that wouldn't be so private. Anyone who was at services would have seen—"

"I understand, but I have to consider what Shelly's wishes might be, and I have no way of knowing, so I err on the side of caution. You understand."

On the short ride back to Geller Investigations, Missy gave Dora a long look. "I'm getting the sense that just about everyone who knew her is hiding something."

Dora pressed her lips together. "And they're hiding the fact that they're hiding something."

Once back at the office, they sat down at Adam's computer, and Missy performed searches in several database application that examined just about every aspect of one's life that required data.

The list included food delivery information, vehicle registration, cell phone users, Internet search engine results, municipal liens and judgments, newspaper articles, and bankruptcy and foreclosure notices. She found several Shelly Borzers, but none were local. She found men with the same or similar names. But she did not find the hairdresser.

• • •

Charlie Bernelli sat in his son C3 and Sarah's living room. Sarah was in the bedroom, feeding Olivia, their two-week-old daughter. Olivia was not taking easily to feeding, and Sarah was trying not to be too upset. She had read that babies with Down syndrome can take longer to adapt to feeding—and to many other things. She and C3 believed they were prepared to deal with whatever issues Olivia was going to face. They would face them together, as a family.

"Do you have any scotch?" Charlie asked his son.

"Dad—I'm sober, in recovery."

Charlie was pacing back and forth, the length of the living room. He was dressed in a gray suit, as he was going from his son and daughter-in-law's apartment to his office for a meeting with a client. C3 sat on the couch, parrying and addressing his father's questions, admonishments, and criticisms. He wore blue jeans and a black polo shirt. Father and son both had longish blond hair; the father's was streaked with gray.

"You do know that babies like Olivia need to be watched for heart defects and hearing and vision issues," Charlie pointed out. "There's a tendency for Down syndrome babies to—"

"Olivia's not a Down syndrome baby," C3 interrupted.

Charlie was frustrated that his son, who had been so volatile his whole life, could be so placid at so critical a moment. "Of course she is!"

"No. That's a label. Olivia's not a label. She's our daughter, and she's a human being. She just happens to have been born with an extra twenty-first chromosome."

Charlie stopped pacing. "Isn't that a label?"

C3 sighed; he was exhausted. He and Sarah had taken turns all night getting up to sit with Olivia who, like many babies, was colicky. She seemed never to sleep, other than periodic dozing during the day.

"We're staying on top of everything, Dad. We're aware of the tendency Olivia may have toward certain conditions. We have a wonderful pediatrician. We're doing all the right things. But more than anything, we're loving our daughter."

Charlie had resumed pacing again and ventured near the door to the bedroom, listening.

"Dad—stop."

Charlie looked at his son. "You sure you haven't got any scotch?"

• • •

Missy looked around for a waiter while Dora took a last look at her menu. They were at Petrocelli's on a Wednesday evening, and the restaurant was rather empty, which, Missy had thought, would likely lead to the wait staff being more available than usual. Apparently, the reverse was true. The wait staff seemed to assume they were less needed than usual and made themselves less available.

"So far," Dora said, looking up from her menu and putting it to one side of her setting, which sat on a linen napkin, "we have a bunch of semi-red flags but nothing actionable." The latter phrase was one often used by Beach City Police Chief Terry Stalwell, a tough but fair leader of local law enforcement, whom Dora liked and admired.

"Right," Missy agreed, taking out her iPhone and opening a Google Doc, where she had listed elements of the case thus far. She began to read. "There's Shelly's last appointment—apparently an emergency with a 90-something-year-old. Then we have tension between the salons, and with the weirdo clients Willa told us about."

"Barbara Skolnick and Kim Lamonte," Dora said, remembering. "Both kind of tough cookie types, but I got no vibe they were hiding anything other than whatever personal stuff they share with their hair stylist. They were being themselves and were happy to talk about having their hair done, if not whatever they confided to Shelly."

"Colorist—not stylist," Missy corrected. "There's also the fact that the salon carries Julienne products, a local company that's been less than pristine."

The waiter, Fabio, arrived with diet sodas for both women, which they had ordered just after sitting down. He then took their order; Dora ordered lasagna and Missy rigatoni *pomodoro*. Both came with side salads.

"So what do you think about moving in together?" Dora asked, after Fabio had departed.

Missy's voice quavered. "Um, let's get back to that," she suggested. "I was wondering what you thought of what we've gone over so far."

Dora's mouth twisted as she considered the question. "Look, they all have possibilities, if we're looking at criminal behavior in a missing persons case, and yet, none gives us anything to lead us to believe that, like, here's the smoking gun. Here's what happened, right?"

"Tell you what jumps out at me," Missy added. "Donnie Schmidt. Now there's a sick guy who's done some criminal stuff."

"Well, but he positively crows about hating Shelly—wanting her dead."

Missy shrugged. "Exactly! Maybe he's a sociopath."

"Maybe, but I don't see him as quite that stupid." The salads arrived. "In my opinion," Dora continued, "the most telling information we've acquired thus far is whatever Father Walt wasn't telling us. Whatever Shelly confided in him. I get the feeling there's a missing puzzle piece here, and we're just not seeing it."

The women enjoyed their salads, followed by the rest of the meal, and split a cannoli for dessert. They never did return to the issue of moving in together.

• • •

Charlie arrived at the Bernelli building in the business district of Beach City, headed into his private office, ignoring the "hello" from his office manager, Vanessa, who was working in the outer office, and went to the bar that was behind a waist level sliding white door in a break-front. His private bar was nearly as well stocked as many commercial bars.

Charlie despaired that his son was now saddled with this lifelong burden, though he had to admit, this burden was the gorgeous, magnetic, sweet new love of his life—his very own granddaughter.

He dealt with this extreme contradiction the only way he knew how. He poured himself a neat scotch, quickly drank it, and poured another. Only then did he venture into the outer office.

"What's happening here?"

Vanessa was petite and attractive; her hair fell about her shoulders and collarbones in golden dreads that were bright against the chestnut tone of her skin. She wore a violet-colored business blouse and a navy skirt with a black belt; her shoes had heels, which were sensible and made for the back-and-forth required of her office work. Her makeup nicely accented her pretty features. "I'm sending another letter to Winchell Garstein," she said. "Taking it up a notch."

Charlie shook his head. His agency produced ads for an upscale local restaurant called The Elegant Lagoon. Garstein was the owner of a New York area music talent agency which sometimes "forgot" to pay its musicians, which led to occasional tension at the venue and, when the problem persisted, fallout that spilled into other business relationships. Garstein liked to push musicians around, as did many venue and talent agency owners. Bad business, Charlie thought, since now, because Garstein was quite late in paying Johnny "Keys" Rabin, a local pianist and vocalist, Rabin had backed out of the next few weeks of gigs at The Elegant Lagoon, which was now losing weekend business—an unnecessary domino effect caused entirely by Garstein's ego.

A few moments later, Charlie's client arrived. Dean Clayburgh Jr. was the thirty-five-year-old owner of HelthE Snax snack foods. His unkempt and unwashed brown hair was long enough to cover his ears and collar—if he had a collar. Clayburgh, however, was wearing a red T-shirt with the logo of a well-known rock band, moccasins, and no socks.

He looked at Charlie's suit and grinned. "Going to a business meeting?"

Swallowing his wounded pride, Charlie grinned back. "Just came from one," he lied.

"What're you driving these days?" Clayburgh asked.

"Twenty-two BMW M3," Charlie answered. He knew what was coming.

"Bought a Lamborghini Huracán EVO six weeks ago. Looking to get rid of it, but there's nowhere to go but down." He shuffled over to the bar and examined its contents. "No single malt?"

Charlie sighed inwardly and opened a cabinet below the bar and retrieved his personal stash of top shelf scotch.

Clayburgh took the bottle and looked at the label. "Did you piss in the bottle or is this really what you drink?"

Without missing a beat, Charlie took the bottle from Clayburgh and began returning it to the cabinet.

"No, no." Clayburgh shook his head, as though allowing himself to be thus demeaned was a personal tragedy. "If you can drink it, it's good enough for me."

"Well, that's kind of you," Charlie said.

"I know," Clayburgh agreed.

Clayburgh's company, HelthE Snax, was a new account for Charlie, one for which he hoped to produce package designs, store displays, shipping containers, and magazine ads. As such, they were of great enough value for Charlie allow for Clayburgh's incessant criticisms and pissing contests.

Clayburgh poured himself a tall single malt while Charlie watched, cringing. They both sat, but Clayburgh bounced up again. "Ooh, I have a surprise for you. You're going to love this."

The buzzer sounded. Charlie stood, frowning. He was not expecting anyone else.

Clayburgh winked. "Right on time! My surprise has arrived." He nodded toward the door, which Charlie opened. An extremely handsome man with finely cut cheekbones, carefully coiffed dark hair, an imported suit and expensive shoes stood in the doorway. When he smiled, twin dimples appeared on either side of his mouth; another in the center of his chin.

"This is Lorne Berger. He's going to be the model for our new ad campaign."

Charlie was surprised. He alone handled all creative aspects of whatever work he produced for his clientele. Here was one of his biggest accounts taking the reins of a creative aspect of work over which he insisted on personal control. Charlie briefly considered arguing with Dean, since a wrong creative choice could harm the man's business. But he decided against speaking up, at least for now, since doing so might negatively impact their relationship going forward.

"Pleasure." He smiled and shook Lorne's hand, briefly wondered about COVID, then led the two men back to his bar, where he let them choose their poison. But Lorne was not looking at the bar; he was facing toward the outer office, where he was staring at Vanessa, who was turned away, bending over a copy machine.

Chapter 7

"Thanks to all our readers," Wally P. said, and everyone applauded. Wally was a hefty man in his late 30s, wearing a red flannel shirt and gold glasses, behind which his eyes were warm and friendly, with more than a hint of humor. Today's meeting consisted of twenty-seven attendees, a good size for this particular AA meeting, especially since it was a Step Meeting—and Step 8, in particular.

"Step 8," Wally read from the poster that was leaned up on a chair at one end of the oval formed by the members' chairs. "'Made a list of all people we have harmed and became willing to make amends to them all.' Who would like to share?" He nodded toward a cinnamon-colored woman with straight, light brown hair that was coiled atop her head.

The woman puffed her cheeks full of air, then blew out a long breath. "Whewww. I'm Keisha, and I'm an alcoholic. I've had a lot of conflict to deal with. I worked a few years at the hospital here in town but lost my job—they said it was for cause, but it was really *'cause* I helped out putting the union together. That was hard work, and I didn't get paid for it. I think I have a right to be pissed off about that! Then I worked at one of the hair salons in town as a colorist—Rainbow Salon, it's called. Is it okay to say that?"

Wally P. shrugged. "You just did."

"Well, that there was pure jealousy. Another colorist, name of Shelly —I won't say her last name, was jealous of me. Of me! And she talked shit about me, so I talked shit back. I don't play like that, and I don't take it when others do. That lady pissed me off. You have no idea." She shook her head.

Wally P. put up his hand. "Point of information—your time's up anyway, Keisha. Step 8 is about making a list of people *we* have harmed, not people who have harmed us."

Keisha's mouth twisted to one side. "Got to give it more thought then." As she spoke, Keisha had looked around the room, connecting to everyone there with her eyes, until they came to rest on a woman dressed in a light blue jumpsuit, a woman with sharp, dark features who was looking at Keisha every bit as hard as Keisha was looking back at Estelle Robinson.

"Typically," Wally P. went on, "we look at our part in each situation, so we can keep our side of the street clean."

Keisha huffed an out breath but didn't say anything more. She and Estelle continued watching one another.

A hand went up. It belonged to a teenage girl with mid-length blond hair that was streaked with red and large brown eyes made up with black eyeliner and mascara, along with heavily applied white goth makeup.

"Lee?"

Lee spoke quickly, anxiously, as though afraid she would not be allowed to get the words out. "Lee, alcoholic. I think about dying a lot. My parents don't accept me as I am, as the person I choose to be, as the person I was born to be." She glanced at Wally P., remembering what he had just said. "So my part in that situation—my part in all of the situations in my life, where people don't accept me for who I am, is that I,

I"—she looked around, as though afraid to speak, then drew herself up, mustering her courage—"I secretly hate them. I wish they were dead." She looked down, and her voice dropped. "I know that's wrong, and I feel bad. So I switch to hating myself. So then…I think a lot about dying." Lee shrugged. "That's it."

The third speaker was Lillian, a small, wiry woman with curly black hair and equally black eyes. Her hands, as usual, were curled into fists; blue veins stood out in her neck. "I work with at risk women—that's my job. And I see all the time how they're treated in the workplace. They're stepped on, used and abused, insulted and fondled. In some cases, they're expected to—"

"No need for a description," Wally quickly cut in.

"Well, you can imagine—put out. Anyway—in terms of Step 8, most of these women never harmed anyone, and if they did, it was well deserved retribution."

"What about you?" asked Wally P.

"Me?" Lillian answered.

"Who have you harmed and owe amends to?"

Lillian's black eyes darted around the room. "Well, maybe my mom. She's seventy-four and in an assisted living facility here in town now. I probably could have been more helpful to her. My father—let's not talk about him. And listen, one thing I've learned at my job—women out there don't feel safe. And they deserve to feel safe. Everybody does."

Another hand went up. "C3?"

"I'm Charles—people call me C3—and I'm an alcoholic. Something a sponsor once told me—this isn't really about making amends. That's in the next step. What we're doing here is just making a list."

Wally P. chuckled. "You're partially correct. We don't need to talk about making any sort of amends here because we'll get to that later. And we *are* making a list. But we are also becoming willing to make amends to them all." The chairperson looked steadily at C3. "This is all about willingness—taking responsibility for hurting others."

C3 nodded and brushed a blond curl from his eyes with a finger. He blew out a long breath. "Well, I guess I've been kind of harsh to my father. He's an alcoholic too. It runs in our family—gallops, in fact."

A few people chuckled.

"And I've blamed him because he hurt us. He hurt our mom, who couldn't take it anymore, and he hurt me. I'm sure he hurt my grandfather, though that may have been a two-way street—I don't know, since he was an alcoholic too, and gone now."

He was about to say something more, but the door opened and C3 sat, mouth open, then said, "Whoa. Speak of the devil."

Charlie Bernelli Jr. had stepped into the room, but he looked over the group, said, "Ahh, shit," turned, and walked back out again.

C3 got up and hurried after his father.

• • •

The brightly lit classroom had been loaned to Women at Risk by the guidance department at Beach City High School. Before entering, Celia Worly nodded to Lillian Walsh, who stood at the doorway and kept track of attendance and managed a variety of other mundane but necessary tasks. She also smiled at William, a hulking, baby-faced young man with developmental disabilities who carried signs, moved chairs and tables, and helped with other physical tasks.

Once inside the classroom, Celia waited as the women began to file in for Wednesday evening's 7:00 p.m. session. She stood at the front of the room, her hands clasped in front of her. She was in her mid-40s, of medium height, with long mahogany-colored hair; her weight was probably more than society's fashionistas would approve of. That was one of her issues with society. Who was anyone else to judge her weight? She was dressed in a smart, white, button-down blouse, light brown slacks and wore an ochre semi-transparent kerchief around her neck. She was in a position of responsibility of sorts here at W.A.R., and she had to look the part.

Between Celia and the chalkboard behind her stood two easels holding two-foot-by-five-foot posters. Both had sky blue backgrounds that were, in fact, photos of a deep azure sky mixed with fluffy white clouds. Pink lettering with deep purple shadowing stood out against the backgrounds of the posters. One poster shouted the headline "Most Common Violence Against Women," below which was a vertical list that read: "Dating violence and abuse; elder abuse; financial abuse; harassment; human trafficking; physical abuse; sexual coercion; stalking; violence against immigrant and refugee women; and violence against women with disabilities." The list had been culled from a government website, as had much of the nonprofit's written and online material. No one was interested in the origins of the organization's materials, however. Everyone there was interested in one thing and one thing only: protecting themselves and other women from being abused and taken advantage of.

The second poster had the headline *The Effects of Violence Against Women*, below which was another list that included physical and emotional injuries, sexual diseases, a variety of traumas—both long and short term, financial suffering, mental health issues, along with employment and school-related issues stemming from abuse. At the bottom of both posters were toll-free phone numbers and the web address and logo of Women at Risk.

Both posters had been made by Lillian, whose talents continued to amaze Celia, who felt she was lucky if she herself could write coherently. Lillian herself was seated off to one side, legs crossed, arms folded across her chest. She was smiling; these were her people, her brood. She and Celia lived to help women at risk.

Celia looked out over the group, all of whom she had come to know by name. She beamed at them all; she knew many quite well: Keisha, Sterling, Suzanne, Myra, Lee, Beth—Shelly was absent today.

"Back when I worked corporate," Celia began, looking the crowd over, "I didn't realize it was wrong for men to grope me. I thought it was okay—that I ought to use whatever assets I might have. I didn't realize that my assets at a corporate job were my business qualifications, my ability to do the job I was hired for, as opposed to giving up my…personal assets to any man who wanted them."

Several of the dozen or so women in attendance nodded in agreement.

"We're here to work together to make your lives, your business circumstances, your homes—wherever you might find yourselves—safe. Women deserve to feel safe, to *be* safe. And that's what Women at Risk is here to help you with, lest anyone have any questions about us."

She looked over the small crowd, waiting for questions, but there were none.

Celia saw Sterling, who sat off to one side, her leg jiggling with anxiety. Sterling and Lee, along with Shelly, had something in common, and were at Woman at Risk for much the same reasons. This was their third class; they had noticed one another and recognized their nearly identical circumstance right away, and struck up a conversation, then a friendship. Lee had recognized Lillian from AA meetings. Sterling did not attend AA, but Lee talked to Sterling about Lillian, assuring her that Lillian was safe and dedicated to their safety as a group. Lee, Sterling, and Shelly needed to be assured of their safety even more than did most women—including women who attended W.A.R.

"Today," Celia continued, "we're going to talk about trends in our legal system. What we are seeing are court cases—not just one, but quite a few, and at every level—cases which cite a man from the seventeenth century—the 1600s!—who was a proponent of the notion that men could have sex with their wives *any time they want to.* That it was impossible, from a legal standpoint, for a man to rape his wife. In some countries—and which ones may surprise you—this is the law of the land. You can rape, excuse me, take sex from your wife, anytime you feel like it. Many courts cite this person from 600 years ago to support and validate ideas that will do anything but make you, as women, safe. Well"—she put her hand to her hips—"what can we do about it? We can take it upon ourselves to keep ourselves safe."

Chapter 8

Detective Gerald Mallard buttoned the top button of his navy blue Prince of Wales suit. The jacket alone had cost him $4400. He smiled at Kay, his wife, who watched him from the kitchen table, sipping her drink and listening to an '80s playlist on Amazon Music. Her dyed blond hair curled above her head and down around her ears, and her complexion was nearly white from refraining from ever leave the house.

"I might be late getting home tonight," he said.

Kay looked at him with mild interest. "Hmm? What?"

Mallard smiled patiently. "Alexa. Softer." The music's volume lowered. "I said—"

"I heard you." She proffered her cheek, and her husband gave it a peck and started for the door, then turned.

"Maybe you should wait until after lunch for your first drink."

Kay looked surprised. She held up her glass for him to see. "This? This is cranberry juice. For female problems."

He looked steadily back at her but decided against responding. Perhaps some small amount of the glass's contents was, in fact, cranberry juice, but what was the point in arguing? Kay would only drink more, and she would drink at him.

Ganderson was waiting outside in a shiny blue Ford Interceptor with all identifying police markings and lights removed, though the car remained easily identifiable as a police vehicle in the way Crown Victorias were identifiable as police vehicles—markings or no.

"Where to?" Mallard asked, as he slid into the passenger seat.

"Barry Hutchins," Ganderson answered. "Where'd you get that suit —a museum?"

Mallard smiled as though the comment were a compliment. "It *is* a collector's item."

Ganderson muttered, "Junk collectors." Mallard pretended he hadn't heard.

They drove five miles north to Sunrise Highway, then west several miles until they reached the southwest section of the Village of Valley Stream, then a two-story private home on Bayview Avenue, a street that was a dead end at both ends; the only access was via two streets with "crest" as part of their names—Lyncrest and Wavecrest—which intersected Bayview at right angles.

Barry Hutchins's address was several doors from an elementary school that lay at the southern end of Bayview Avenue. As the two detectives approached the front door, it was opened before they had a chance to knock by a boy in his early teens.

"We're looking for Barry Hutchins," Ganderson said.

The boy turned. "Daaad!" he sang.

The man who came to the door was short and stocky and wore green chinos and an off-white collared shirt with faint blue pinstripes. He had neatly trimmed brown hair and small green eyes that hinted at curiosity and intelligence. "Police officers?"

"Barry Hutchins?" Mallard asked.

The man nodded. "What's this about?"

"May we come in?" Mallard asked.

"Is everything okay?" Hutchins asked anxiously. "It's not my wife, is it? The turn signal on the Impala's been broken nearly a week, and we were going to—she wasn't in an accident—" He staggered back two steps.

"No, sir. This is not about your wife." Mallard held up a hand and nodded toward the interior of the home. Hutchins took a few deep breaths and stepped aside, allowing the detectives to enter.

The living room was nicely furnished, with stained but worn wood floors, thin beige striped oval throw rugs, and light tan painted walls adorned with framed paintings of flowers and still lifes that added some color to the room. Smaller frames held photos of the boy who had answered the door, a girl of about eight, a woman who was presumably the children's mother, and Hutchins.

Hutchins nodded to a sofa; the detectives sat. He saw them looking at the paintings. "Wife likes flowers," he said.

"Nothing wrong with flowers," Mallard answered. Ganderson looked pointedly disinterested.

"Coffee?"

Now Ganderson looked interested. "That would be great."

"Milk? Cream? Sugar? I have Splenda." Hutchins looked at them both.

"Black," they said simultaneously.

Hutchins made two trips to the kitchen while the detectives looked around. He set the coffees for his guests on napkins on a glass coffee table while Ganderson got up to examine the family photos. Hutchins returned with his own coffee, set it on a napkin, and sat down in a high-backed brown velour armchair at right angles to the detectives' chairs. Hutchins leaned forward, his elbows on his knees, and waited.

"Mr. Hutchins," Mallard began. "Do you know a Steven Berger?"

Hutchins's eyebrows went up, and he tipped his head to one side. "My best friend." He paused. "Well, he was. We've been out of touch for a while."

"How long a while?" Ganderson asked, returning from the photos and taking a seat.

Hutchins looked toward the ceiling. "Four, maybe five years. Maybe more. Let's see…" He looked at the two detectives, who could see he was trying to place his memories in time. "The last time we played paddleball was right around Anita—that's my daughter—right around Anita's third birthday. We had a party, and Steven attended. So that would be just over five years ago this past August."

"Why did you lose touch?" Mallard asked while Ganderson sipped his coffee, his eyes on Hutchins.

"Good question," came the answer. "I honestly don't know. Steven —how do I explain this? Steven changed. I stopped hearing from him, and he stopped taking my calls. He had become sort of withdrawn. He'd gotten into drinking instead of playing paddleball—sometimes just before playing—which was surprising. Steven loved paddleball. Took it seriously—said it kept him sane. Maybe he was right. Maybe he had an injury, couldn't play paddleball, and lost it." He looked at the detectives to see what they thought of his theory.

Ganderson stared back at him. Mallard nodded.

Hutchins shook his head. "In any case, that was before our daughter's party. Soon after we had breakfast a couple of times. He seemed to have stopped drinking—I remember being relieved to hear that, though I wasn't sure I believed him. But then, he just—disappeared. Fell off the face of the earth—never took another of my calls. Eventually I got a message that he was no longer at that number. Moved or became a hermit, far as I could tell."

"Did you try going to his place?" Mallard asked.

Hutchins shook his head. "Maybe I should have, but I didn't." He looked mildly embarrassed.

"And this was five years ago?" Mallard sipped his coffee. "This is delicious, but the way."

"Thank you," said Hutchins, nodding in answer to the question. "I do remember one thing—because it was, well, weird, quite frankly." Hutchins shook his head, his mouth twisting. "He began going to these art shows."

"Art shows," Mallard repeated.

"Right. He dragged me along once, and it was the most boring afternoon of my life." He stroked his chin. "But...he'd become friendly with a sort of alternative lifestyle crowd—people who, on the surface seemed completely normal, but were...weird."

"Weird like, how?" Ganderson asked.

"Not sure how to describe it."

Somewhere in the distance, police sirens—several of them—sounded. Mallard could see Ganderson listening to them, as though trying to discern details.

"They were just… different. Not themselves…"

"What does that mean?" Ganderson asked.

"Did they seem as though they might have been engaged in…criminal activity?" Mallard wanted to know. Ganderson looked at him, annoyed that he'd asked another question before his own was fully answered.

"Oh, no!" Hutchins responded. "They seemed to be perfectly good people. I know that at least some of them went to church. We spoke about it, in fact." He gave a small smile. "About all I had in common with the ones I talked to. They were involved in a number of local charities. But they were just…different."

Ganderson leaned forward. "You say your friend changed. How?"

Hutchins tightened his jaw and his lower lip curled outward. "Different clothes, for one thing."

"Different?"

"He suddenly took to scarves. And earrings, and he grew his hair. And sort of frilly clothes. And eventually…makeup."

"Makeup?" Ganderson repeated. Hutchins nodded.

"Did you have reason to believe your friend had…some sort of alternative lifestyle?" Mallard asked.

"Or alternative life," Ganderson added.

Hutchins looked sharply at them both. He slowly nodded. "Maybe."

• • •

Missy moved to the back seat of Dora's car to make room for Lieutenant Trask, who had met them around the corner from the police station. Trask got into the front seat and said, "Drive."

Dora obliged. "Thank you for talking to us," she said.

Trask took a breath and looked out the window. "Yeah, well…"

"You really used to date Detective Ganderson?" Missy asked. She was picturing the taciturn senior detective with the diminutive, usually easy-going lieutenant.

Trask laughed. "Date? Not the word I'd use. Let's say we didn't part the best of friends, hence my willingness to discuss, even though it might hurt Mallard's close rate. Mallard's a pain in the ass, but he's harmless—and a pretty good detective." She thought for a moment. "As is Ganderson. It's just that he's an asshole. So let's move it along."

"Fair enough," Dora agreed.

"So," Trask continued, "no one has reported Shelly Borzer missing, nor has anyone turned up that fits her description. We currently have three open missing persons cases. A Ralph Baker, who's ninety-three and was reported missing only this morning. Seems he wandered out of a senior facility."

"Don't they lock the doors?" Missy asked.

"They do," Trask confirmed, shrugging. "As boomers age, this sort of thing is only going to get worse. What can I tell you? Then there's a Chandra Chappelle, who we suspect is a runaway. She's twenty-three and has run away before."

"But came back," Dora pointed out.

"Well, she did, but there's been nothing but trouble in her household. Everyone's forever beating up everyone else, and someone's forever calling us. Some families are like that."

"Tell me about it," Dora agreed.

"I just did," Trask said. "Then there's Steven Berger, who was last seen five years ago by his only sibling, his brother Lorne. Berger's only real friend, a Barry Hutchins, also hasn't seen or heard from Steven in years. And none of our searches gave us anything besides information from around that time."

"DMV?" Dora asked.

"They have his driver's license, but that hasn't led to anything actionable," Trask answered. "And they asked around at his old haunts—bars and restaurants, neighbors. All came up empty. Something must have happened either in his personal life or internally—emotionally, you know?"

"Why do you say that?" asked Missy from the back seat.

"His style of dress changed. And his personal grooming."

"Huh," said Missy.

"How so?" Dora asked.

Lieutenant Trask explained.

Chapter 9

The next day, Dean Clayburgh showed up again, and Charlie took his presence as an omen. He decided that he was meant to go drinking with the client rather than to AA with his son—or where he might run into his son. So Charlie and Clayburgh had a few fingers of top shelf scotch and headed off to The Gold Standard, a local restaurant that marketed itself as so elegant and priced its fare so high that their clientele were few and far between and very, very wealthy.

Vanessa Burrell was alone at the office, doing "service," which involved collating the notes from Charlie's meetings thus far with Clayburgh and several other clients and turning them into specific instructions for their designer, Luis Martinez, who had been mostly working from home since the advent of COVID just over two years ago.

Vanessa was startled by the unexpected knock on the office door, which opened to reveal the handsome face of their newly hired model, Lorne Berger. He gave Vanessa a shy, questioning smile, code for "Is it okay to come in?"

Appreciating the implied assurance of safety, she gave him a warm, welcoming smile in return, and Lorne stepped fully into the office. He was wearing a maroon blazer, a long-sleeved purple dress shirt with gold cufflinks, sleek brown slacks, and Italian loafers sans socks. Twin gold chains twinkled around his neck.

"I happened to be in the neighborhood and couldn't help but see Dean and your boss heading out, and I thought—"

"You'd head in," Vanessa finished for him, laughing.

"Well—" Lorne smiled sheepishly. "I thought you might like dinner."

Vanessa's eyes narrowed. "Because you…happened to be in the neighborhood?"

He shrugged and held up a violet umbrella. "It's raining a bit, but I'm nothing if not prepared."

Vanessa wondered if Lorne's look of embarrassment was feigned, perhaps even practiced. She suspected he was more prepared than he let on but decided it didn't matter. She was unabashedly attracted to the man's ridiculously good looks and undeniable charm. She hadn't slept with a man since she'd lost Jesse what seemed like a lifetime ago—and she was famished.

Over cocktails, followed by mussels marinara, rigatoni a la vodka, and a bottle of merlot, all of which they shared, Vanessa told Lorne the sad story of Jesse's murder and her ensuing struggle to raise their two boys, who were now eight and nearly five. Lorne made all the right sounds of compassion and sympathy.

After dinner, they rose to leave, and Vanessa stumbled slightly. "Stupid office shoes." She sent Lorne an embarrassed smile. "I don't do well in heels."

Lorne extended an arm, bent at the elbow. "Let me escort you to your door. Feel free to take them off."

Vanessa gratefully slipped her shoes off, held them with one hand, took Lorne's arm with the other, and they walked out into the spring night, where the rain must have just stopped, leaving the air moist, cool and refreshing.

They arrived at the entrance to Vanessa's building, and Lorne stopped and stepped back. "Thank you for a wonderful evening," he said. "Nicest time I've had in I don't know how long."

Vanessa cocked her head slightly to the right. "Why don't you—why don't you come in for coffee?"

Lorne agreed. "I do have a bit of a drive."

Vanessa knew this wasn't true but said nothing and put an index finger to her lips as they entered the apartment. "Hopefully the boys are sleeping." The couple paused inside the doorway.

Dora, who had been babysitting Vanessa's sons, Drew and Buster, was sitting on the couch, looking into her phone. She stood up as Vanessa and Lorne approached.

"Boys okay?" Vanessa asked.

"We looked at Leo and talked about his story. Now they're out like lights."

Vanessa looked at Lorne. "My boys love astronomy."

"Ah," Lorne said with a beatific grin. "'Silently, one by one, in the infinite meadows of heaven, blossomed the lovely stars, the forget-me-nots of the angels.'" For a moment, no one said anything, then Lorne said, "Longfellow."

"Whoa." Vanessa practically swooned. "Excuse me, I need to check on the boys." She put a hand on Lorne's forearm, turned and stepped from the room.

"How do you know Vanessa?" Dora asked.

"I was hired by her company to model for some snack food ads."

"Believe it or not," said Dora, "I modeled for a tourism campaign Charlie ran a year and a half ago. It was a Rosie the Riveter type of thing —saying regular people, not just model types, can enjoy summers here in Beach City." She gave Lorne a pointed look. "No offense."

Lorne laughed politely.

Vanessa returned and grinned at Dora. "Whatever you do, it's like a tranquilizer." She turned to Lorne. "I have hyperactive boys. They're like two rocket ships. Oh, I'm sorry, I didn't introduce you two. Dora Ellison, my boys' babysitter, part time model and private investigator extraordinaire, meet Lorne Berger, model and, apparently, terrific guy."

Dora and Lorne shook hands. Lorne held on to Dora's hand a moment longer than necessary. "Private investigator?"

"Next time." Vanessa had taken Dora by the arm and was leading her to the door. As she opened the door and Dora stepped into the doorway, she turned and saw Vanessa wink and giggle.

The door shut, and Dora stood alone in the hallway for a long moment, thinking. Puzzle pieces were snapping into place.

• • •

It was just after 9:30 p.m. when Lee Travers walked along the deserted street, staying just on the street side of the curb, so as to walk under the streetlights, which were two to a block and only on her side of the street. She was often out at night, walking to and from friends' homes, group or any number of appointments, which were usually scheduled for the evening because she was still in school.

She was enjoying the remnants of what had been a lovely spring day —air that had been warmed by bright sunshine, the daffodils, crocuses, and tulips that adorned many of the properties along the residential street, and the faint smell of honeysuckle that took her back to an early childhood of bike riding and active sports so often played along streets not so different from this one.

She had noticed the black pickup truck a half block before, first as an unnamed presence following her a half block behind, then as a hulking black shape rumbling along the path she had just walked, maintaining its distance. She heard the truck before she saw it, and when she did see it, she saw only a moving piece of dark night.

Her mind was filled with the echoes of her experience of only minutes before—the voices, the information, the laughter, the friendship— and so at first she didn't notice when the truck accelerated suddenly to only a few feet behind her. When she did, she turned to run, but for Lee, it was too late. A figure was out of the car and calling to her. Then, a series of quick, staccato shots, and Lee's last awareness was of the familiar-yet-fading voice, along with the sweet smell of honeysuckle on this otherwise fine spring night.

• • •

Dora looked at Missy as they sat beside the computer in the back of Geller Investigations. "I have an idea."

"Uh oh!" called Thelma, in a voice somewhere between a croak and a bellow. "Better hide under your desks."

"Thank you, Thelma," Dora replied.

"Ah, my wit is lost on you kids. You didn't live through the sixties."

Dora and Missy gave one another confused looks.

Dora stood up.

"Where are we going?" Missy asked as she followed.

"City Hall."

City hall sat at the far end of a half block wide and deep town square that was home to concerts, art exhibitions, and farmers' markets during the warm weather. The building itself was a six-story brick structure whose front façade was undergoing renovation and was currently covered with scaffolding. Above the scaffolding were five stories of dark blue tinted floor-to-ceiling windows. Along the east side of the building were a half dozen parked black and white police vehicles.

From behind a protective glass, John smiled at their approach. "How are you, young lady? Out there fighting crime?"

Dora laughed. "I'm good. You know Missy Winters."

John nodded. "I know of her, and I recognize her from the last time you were here—when you refrained from introducing us, I might add." He grinned at Missy. "I also recognize you from your picture in the *Chronicle*, which doesn't do you justice."

Missy blushed as John tapped the side of his face. "Masks, ladies."

They complied.

"Now where are you two headed?"

"Clerk's office."

"You know where it is."

The administrative area of the clerk's office was behind a dark wood veneer half-wall that was topped by a blue faux marble countertop that separated civil servants from the public. Behind the wall and to one side was a row of five cubby office spaces, separated by chest-high portable dividers. The other side was filled with filing cabinets, the contents of which were in the long process of being transferred to digital servers.

Dora had stopped working for the city a year and a half earlier, so she knew only one of the assistant clerks behind the counter. That clerk, a short, thin, bony man named James, greeted her with a smile.

"Officer Ellison!"

Dora looked embarrassed. "You know I left the program, Jimmy."

James shrugged. "To move onward and upward in the world of private practice."

"Is Robin around?"

"Hang on." James turned and walked back to a doorway on the left side of the admin area, knocked on the open door, and said a few words *sotto voce*.

Robin Torsch was in her early forties, with long, sun-bleached blonde hair and a year-round tan. Her smile was ever-present and professional. She rarely spoke with members of the public, preferring the privacy of her office and communication by text and email, but the previous clerk, now the mayor, Christine Pearsall, considered Dora a valued friend, so Robin made it her business to welcome Dora into her rarified professional inner circle.

The clerk nodded politely to Missy and addressed Dora. "Nice to see you. How can I help?"

"What can you tell me about the person who lives at this address?" She opened a Google Doc in her phone and read Robin the address Sawyer Townsend had provided as Shelly Borzer's.

Robin hesitated, and Dora could see that she was uncomfortable with the request. Perhaps she was waiting to see if Dora would change her mind. She would not. Dora waited, and Robin blinked and went to one of the file cabinets along the wall. She returned with a manilla folder.

"One of these days we'll digitize everything and who knows what we'll do with all this space."

Dora smiled as Robin opened the file.

"The property is owned by a Lucio Tavarino and is currently rented to a Steven Berger, who, by the way, has three outstanding parking tickets. All in the last year, to a 2021 Volvo XC40. White with black top and trim. Plug-in hybrid no less." She looked up. "That's all we have on the guy." She looked steadily at Dora, who realized she was expected to thank Robin and leave.

Dora gave the clerk a polite smile. "Much appreciated. Come on, Miss."

Chapter 10

Ganderson and Mallard, a.k.a. the Goose and the Gander, arrived at the medical examiner's office twenty minutes after being summoned. They would have arrived sooner, but Ganderson had been at a local deli, enjoying a bowl of hot chicken noodle soup, his favorite, and given the call was not exactly an emergency since the victim was already deceased, he insisted on waiting until he had finished before meeting Mallard, who was already on his way.

Once they arrived, the ME's conservatively dressed assistant, Margaret Blufeld, led the two detectives into a medical suite that was empty, save for a young person's naked body that lay on a table.

A bag nearby contained torn green and blue fabrics that had been the person's clothing.

From the center of the torso up, the body was intact. From the stomach down to the thighs, the body had been torn apart—wounds the detectives recognized as having come from a semi-automatic rifle.

Moments later, Dr. Roger Ravell waddled into the room; he was a heavy man in his early fifties, bald except for a short fringe of light brown hair with encroaching gray roots around the sides and back of the top of his head.

"Ah," he said. "I see you've met Lee."

Mallard wrinkled his nose at the smell and at the sight of the victim's mutilated genital area. Ganderson glanced at the body, then at the ME, who was shaking his head.

"What a mess—poor guy."

Ganderson looked surprised. "This is a guy?"

Ravell nodded. "Was. Made up to look like a woman. Did some other things too, but this is a young man, though I understand it's politically correct to use whatever pronoun the individual prefers. I'm guessing that's she or her, in this case—not to be confusing."

"Weapon?" Mallard asked, ignoring the rest.

Ravell looked gravely at the detectives. "High-powered semi-automatic rifle—probably an AR-15, firing hollow points. They're all over the criminal landscape."

"Huh," Mallard said.

Ravell began to walk back and forth beside the body.

Ganderson whistled. "Like what cannon balls did to soldiers in the Revolutionary War."

Ravell shook his head. "This is worse. The velocity devastates everything—skin, bone, tissue, clothes. A bullet from an AR-15 travels nearly three times as fast as a nine millimeter round." His mouth twisted with regret. "The damage spreads outward, way beyond the trajectory of the bullet."

Mallard pressed his lips together. "Makes for big exit wounds."

"Anyway," the doctor said, "this is either Lee or Leonard Travers, depending on whether you believe the driver's license or the credit cards in the clutch purse she was carrying."

Now both Ganderson and Mallard took a more careful look at the victim, whose features, musculature, and lack of facial hair were androgynous, if not female, in appearance, and whose makeup was that of a woman.

"You're sure this is a guy?" Ganderson said, glancing toward the ravaged genital area.

Dr. Ravell nodded. "Was. Given the wounds, I had to do a partial autopsy to be sure, but yes. The killer apparently tried to disguise that fact, if not change it completely. Though of course, I couldn't speculate as to motive, other than to kill and maim. The why—couldn't say."

The victim was a teenager with shoulder-length reddish blonde hair, thick black eyeliner and mascara, and heavily applied white goth facial powder or cream.

"He, or she, may have undergone some hormonal therapy, as there is evidence of breast development, lack or reduction of facial hair, and smooth muscles that might come with androgen deprivation therapy and possibly estrogen or progestin."

Ganderson pursed his lips. "So you're saying this is a guy who was turning himself into a woman?"

Ravell shrugged, slid his glasses down his nose, and looked over them at Ganderson. "I'm not saying what the victim's intentions were in that regard—only that this is or was a young man who seems to be dressed and made up as a woman and who appears to have undergone hormonal treatment that may or may not have been part of a gender tran-sition."

Mallard was rubbing his chin thoughtfully between a thumb and forefinger and shaking his head. "Not listed as a missing person, unless it just came in."

Ganderson chewed the inside of his cheek and kept glancing at, then away from, the genital wounds. "Someone's got quite the screw loose. Wonder where the kid's parents are, why they haven't reported her... him."

"Maybe he lived on his own," Mallard offered.

Ganderson looked at his partner, then at the victim, still chewing, and didn't answer.

• • •

Dora lay in the sun on the roof of the 47th floor of the building in sunny Rio de Janeiro. Next to her was Andressa Cardoso, the UFC fighter and recently dethroned champion. Both were nude. Two thoughts converged, and a revelation bloomed. An enormous fly buzzing around them interrupted her thinking and clouded her mind. She tried to return to the revelation, but the fly buzzed incessantly in concentric circles around her head, each circle closer than the last.

She opened her eyes and turned her head. She was in her bed; Missy was beside her. They were both in pajamas. The revelation was one that had been nagging at her but had stayed just out of reach until now.

She knew more about Steven Berger than she thought. In fact, Steven Berger had a best friend and a brother, and she and Missy had been told about both by Lieutenant Trask. She had even met the brother—Vanessa's new paramour, Lorne Berger, who had been trying to locate this brother, Steven. When Lieutenant Trask had explained to her about Berger's friend, Barry Hutchins, she had mentioned Lorne.

The pieces were coming together but were not quite making sense. Why was Steven Berger renting an apartment in Shelly Borzer's name, and what did the two have to do with one another? Did they have a relationship? Were they related? Roommates?

But the buzzing would not stop. She sat up and looked down at Missy; the girl could sleep through anything! She threw on a T-shirt and shorts, not bothering with underwear, and rushed outside.

She found a man in his mid 30s walking back and forth on the driveway, sidewalk and street of the house next door, his leaf blower blasting. There were no leaves to be seen.

Dora waved her hand toward either end of the neighbor's property. "No leaves!"

He shook his head, frowning, indicating he could not hear her.

"I'll make you hear me!" She pulled the leaf blower from his hands and tried to wrestle it away from him, but the device was held on by a strap that went around his shoulder. Still gripping the barrel end of the blower, she spun him around, slid the device from his body, and pounded it against the ground, where it coughed a few times, sputtered, and died.

• • •

Officer Paul Miller was a fit new member of the force with short, sandy brown hair, an olive complexion, and a ramrod bearing. He had a habit of clenching his jaw when concentrating. Mallard thought of his dentist and wondered if Miller had grinding problems that caused him dental issues; maybe he had a mouth guard for nighttime use.

Now Miller stood next to Ganderson and Mallard's desks, hands clasped behind his back, bouncing on his toes, obviously anxious to make a good impression. Mallard suspected this was the young man's first contact with a real homicide.

"Just tell us what you saw," Ganderson said.

"Don't worry," Mallard encouraged, "your training will fill in blanks."

The new officer gave a quick nod, then squinted, remembering.

"The victim was found under the boardwalk, in the crevice where the boardwalk first rises at the west end. You saw the photos, so you know about body placement. We found no murder weapon. There were drag marks and minimal blood, so obviously the murder occurred elsewhere. Since this is where the boardwalk slopes down to meet the ground, it's not a place anyone would go, as no one would fit in there except perhaps a child who's hiding—playing hide 'n seek, maybe. This is a place someone is stashed. Whatever the weapon was tore the body up."

"AR-15," Mallard said.

Ganderson turned and looked steadily at him as if to say, "Why did you need to say that?" Mallard ignored him.

Miller continued. "Citizen named Alicia Garcia found him. She was walking her dog around 7:00 a.m. I took her statement, which you have."

No one said anything for a moment, then Ganderson said, "Thank you, Miller."

Miller waited a moment, glanced at Mallard, then left.

Ganderson looked at Mallard. "You don't need to tell him what he doesn't need to know."

Mallard looked right back at his partner. "No, I didn't need to tell him anything. I chose to. I tell them things so they'll learn." They stared at once another.

Then Ganderson said, "Ravell said time of death was about six hours prior to the body being found."

"So around midnight," Mallard reasoned. "Maybe slightly before. That's one loud weapon. We'll canvas the area to see if anything or anyone was seen or heard."

Ganderson shrugged. "The sound of the surf and bikes on the boardwalk, even at that hour, would cover much. Bikes make a crisp clacking sound on that boardwalk."

Mallard shook his head. "But not as rapid fire as the AR-15 and lacking that deep punch."

"Yeah, well," Ganderson equivocated. "Given the drag marks in this woman's report, I don't suppose the murder took place near that beach entrance, where the marks start. This could have been done anywhere.

We need to find out who would know this person, whether anyone knows they're missing, where they've been, and with whom."

Mallard nodded. "Agreed—and whether anyone in the vicinity saw anything."

• • •

"No, no, no! We want to see those beautiful abs alongside the packaging!" Dean Clayburgh bounded out of his chair and hurried past Charlie and Ramon, the videographer, who had been circling Lorne, who wore a pair of distressed jeans and nothing else. He had been holding a colorful bag of HelthE Snax Mix next to his chest. Clayburgh gently lowered Lorne's hands and his product so that they were next to the model's stomach, which he then gently brushed with the tips of the fingers of his right hand. "Ooh. I like." He turned to look at Charlie, who was waiting patiently, and smiled. "You may proceed."

The photo and video shoot continued, with Luis, the designer, at a desk off to one side, where he was working on ad comps and receiving photo and video files from Ramon every few minutes. After just over an hour, everyone congregated behind Luis's desk and gazed at his computer screen.

"Ooh, I like that!" Dean cooed, his voice muffled slightly; he had his own open bag of HelthE Snax in one hand, into which he dipped his other every now and then, stuffing his mouth with the product. "These really do have health benefits," he said, "only the FDA makes us change

102

the spelling of the product name because we don't meet *their* arbitrary standards." His tone was disdainful. He looked at the crumbling mix of ingredients in his fist and shook his head with loving wonder. "Chock full of goodness!"

. . .

During the shoot, Vanessa had been running the office, making and receiving calls from clients and prospects, making appointments for Charlie, handling production issues with printers and Internet vendors and approving and amending designs. Michele had been the office manager prior to Vanessa's arrival and was now Vanessa's assistant. Charlie had immediately seen that Vanessa had managerial if not executive potential, and elevated her to office manager, with an eye toward possible future executive advancement. If Michele was perturbed by Vanessa's leapfrogging, she never showed it. Under Vanessa Burrell's multifaceted direction, The Bernelli Group's office ran smoothly, efficiently and profitably.

At the end of the day, she found Lorne waiting for her in the lobby.

"Does Charlie know about us?" he asked her.

She shrugged. "If I know Charlie, which I do, he doesn't care—long as business is done and the clients are happy—and I'm happy."

Fifteen minutes later, they walked into Vanessa's apartment, where Dora was sitting in front of the living room coffee table, doing a puzzle which lay next to a crumpled bag of HelthE Snax.

"The boys are fast asleep. We looked at Virgo tonight—goddess of justice and the harvest."

Vanessa shook her head in wonder and glanced at Lorne. "I try to do constellations with them, but they don't sleep." She turned to Dora. "You've got to show me how you do it."

"Easy," Dora replied. "I'm not their mother. They think they can pull off the stay-up-late routine with you, so they do. Not happening with me."

"You like puzzles?" Lorne asked, noticing the puzzle on the coffee table and the unused pieces beside it.

"Obsessed with them," Dora said. "In fact, I have sort of a puzzle question for you." She looked at Vanessa, who gave a "why not" shrug. "So," she said, "you know I'm a private investigator."

Lorne said, "I remember."

"I've been investigating a missing person, a hair colorist named Shelly Borzer, and learned that Steven Berger, your brother, has been renting an apartment in her name. The police are looking for Steven, as you know."

"I asked them to. He's been named in our mother's will."

Dora and Vanessa waited, but Lorne didn't continue.

"I have a theory," Dora added. "I suspect that Shelly Borzer and your brother, Steven Berger, are the same person."

No one said anything for a moment. Then Lorne said, "When I hadn't heard anything from the police, I started doing my own investigating, and I think you might be right."

Vanessa said, "I don't understand. She uses his name to rent?"

"I don't think so," Dora said. "I think Shelly Borzer is a woman who used to be Steven Berger."

Lorne nodded slowly. "Isn't that interesting?"

"Given that," Dora continued, looking steadily at Lorne, "do you have any clue where she might be?"

Lorne quickly shook his head. "No idea."

Chapter 11

The detectives arrived at a faded white Victorian house surrounded by a gray wooden porch from which an old green couch, two rickety rocking chairs, and a half dozen cheap, pine folding chairs looked out onto the street. Inside, they found six young men and three women, along with their house supervisor, Wally Peterson, waiting in a study, surrounded by shelves containing old, used books.

Ganderson surveyed the room. "Is this the residence of Lee Travers?"

Everyone looked at Peterson, who nodded. "But she hasn't been here in a while."

"Yeah, we know."

Peterson looked confused. "So why are you here?"

"We'll ask the questions." Ganderson squared his stance and faced the house supervisor. "When's the last time any of you saw her?"

"Three days ago, when she went to her women's group—a place called Women at Risk. She never came back."

"Any idea where she might have gone?" Mallard asked, his eyes scanning the group.

No one answered; several residents shook their heads.

"Do your residents make a habit of just running off?" Ganderson inquired sharply.

Peterson smiled, as did some of the residents.

"Something funny?" Mallard asked; the smiles faded.

"Actually, sir, they do," Peterson answered. "It's pretty common. Guys are trying to get clean—and it's difficult. Sometimes they just go off, find what they need and a place to do it. That's the end of them as far as we know."

"Then what?" Mallard asked.

Peterson shrugged. "Some end up in jail or in detox, if they have insurance. Who knows?" He shrugged again. "Some die. That's the system."

"Some system," Mallard observed. "So does anyone here know Lee well enough to tell us more about her?" He looked over the group, several of whom had turned toward a teen with scraggly black hair, a long face riddled with acne, a dirty white T-shirt and greasy shorts that might have once been black. The boy slowly raised a shaky hand.

Mallard looked at the boy. "What's your name, son?"

"Doug, sir." The boy did not look directly at Mallard, but at a spot to the side of the detective's left ear.

"Is there someplace we can go?" Ganderson asked the supervisor.

Peterson nodded. "How's the porch?"

"One thing," Ganderson interrupted. "Can you think of anyone, who for any reason, might have wanted to hurt Lee?"

Silence. Ganderson took out a card and handed it to Peterson. "If anyone thinks of anything, they can contact us directly—and no one needs to know."

After a moment's hesitation, the boys disbursed with curious glances at their compatriot, who accompanied the detectives outside, where they took seats on the porch.

"How old is Lee?" Ganderson interrupted.

"Sixteen, sir."

"Has she ever been in trouble?"

"Not to my knowledge, sir."

"Tell us about your friend," Mallard suggested. "She was your friend, wasn't she?"

The boy's eyes filled with tears. "Was, sir? She was my best friend."

Ganderson was looking daggers at his partner, who glanced away, realizing his mistake.

The detectives did not address the implied question, but waited.

Doug explained. "Lee loved to play soccer, but never made the team at school. She was an okay student. Liked history, but was pretty good in all her classes—except math. She hated math." The boy laughed, then caught himself and stopped.

"Tell me," Ganderson began, "was Lee technically a girl? I mean did she change…" He waved his hand in a vague circle.

"I don't know. I don't think so. She'd had some hormone therapy." Doug gave a faint smile. "She wanted to be a teacher, maybe a high school history teacher, or even a college professor." The boy looked at his feet, which had been swinging and bumping the couch. "She won't get to do that, will she?"

"No, son. She won't." Mallard gently admitted, drawing another frustrated glance from Ganderson.

"Who did she spend her time with?"

"Me, mostly. She also went to W.A.R." He clenched his jaw.

Ganderson squinted. "What do you mean? She had violent tendencies?"

Doug laughed. "As if. It's a women's group—Women at Risk."

"Women at Risk. W.A.R.," Mallard repeated. "Anything else you can tell us?"

Doug shrugged.

Mallard took out one of his cards and handed it to the young man. "If you think of anything else, call us. Day or night. And you don't have to tell Peterson."

"When do you sleep?" the boy asked.

Mallard smiled, as the detectives rose and walked to their car.

"Yeah," Ganderson repeated. "When *do* you sleep?"

• • •

Dora and Missy had just returned from a walk with both their dogs and were doing their preferred brainwork—Missy a Sudoku and Dora a puzzle—at Missy's apartment when Dora's phone rang. She saw it was from "Beach City Police," so she took the call, which was from Lieutenant Catherine Trask.

"Dora, could you come down here, please? We have a bit of a situation you need to clear up."

"To the station?"

"That's right."

"Sure."

"I'm coming with you," Missy insisted.

Dora gave her a long look. "You can wait in the car until I find out what's going on."

"Why?"

"Just…because."

Fifteen minutes later, Dora walked through the main entrance of the police station and was buzzed in by Lieutenant Morse, who simply said, "Chief."

Dora knocked on Chief Terry Stalwell's door, which was open. She could see the chief and his second-in-command, Captain Richard "The Dick" Waycrest, a tall, lean man with close cropped dark hair going gray on the sides, small eyes that moved independently of his body, and a perpetual scowl.

As she entered, Waycrest turned to face her. "You have the right to remain silent—"

"What?" She looked at the chief, a dignified looking man whose dark brown face was normally kindly, but today was decidedly not.

"Hang on, Dick," the chief said, then turned to Dora. "I have a complaint that you assaulted a gardener and vandalized equipment."

"What? I—ohhh…"

"Yeah," Waycrest repeated, sarcastically, "oh!"

Stalwell sighed. "Close the door, Dick."

Dora glared at the assistant chief. "Yeah, *Dick.*"

Stalwell waved a finger at her, then at Waycrest. "Stop it. Both of you!"

Waycrest's features were clenched. Saliva had collected in a corner of his mouth. "She's guilty! As good as admitted it!"

"Shut up!" the chief barked. For a moment, no one spoke. "You destroyed a piece of a gardener's equipment."

"I was sleeping. It was early in the morning, and he was using one of those stupid leaf blowers."

"How early?" the chief demanded.

"I don't know."

"How early?"

"Maybe…nine thirty."

"Landscape artists can use their equipment," Waycrest said, "after eight, except on Sunday, when it's nine."

"Landscape artists?" Dora laughed. "Is that what that guy calls himself?"

The chief rubbed the sides of his mouth between his fingers. "First of all, Dora, you could be arrested for assault."

Waycrest glared, widening his eyes at her; Dora tried to ignore him.

"As it is, you scared the crap out of the poor guy, who quit then and there."

Dora laughed.

"It isn't funny," the chief admonished. "Really! We don't condone violence or the threat of it. Period. Zero tolerance."

Dora gritted her teeth and nodded. "Yes, sir."

"Is that it?" Waycrest was incredulous.

"No, that's not it." The chief looked at Dora levelly. "Intentionally damaging the property of another person is criminal mischief in the fourth degree and a class A misdemeanor."

"She should do time!" Waycrest insisted.

Chief Stalwell blew out a breath. "She will not do time. She will, however, make restitution and apologize—both in person and in writing, to the individual and his former employer."

Dora didn't answer.

"I didn't hear you," Stalwell said.

"Yes, sir."

"Next time," he continued, "and there will not be a next time—you *will* do time."

Dora returned to the car and reluctantly explained to Missy what had just taken place.

"Look," Missy said, "I don't like leaf blowers either, but when you destroyed that thing, you destroyed the guy's livelihood. And who were you really angry at, anyway?"

"The guy with the leaf blower. Who do you think?"

Missy shook her head; Dora could see the disappointment in her eyes. "The guy's just trying to make a living. Are you angry at the guy who hired him? At the homeowner?"

"I don't know. Give it a rest, Miss."

They drove back to Dora's apartment in silence.

As they parked, Dora turned to Missy. "You know, both our dogs are rescues. Because of that, they're jumpy. They flip out. In a way, I'm a rescue too." She widened her eyes at Missy, who didn't answer. "Think about it."

• • •

The W.A.R. office was a single room above an insurance broker. The door from the second-floor landing was made of flimsy, aged pine with a grid of eight windows that ran from just above eye level for Mallard to mid-thigh level. The door had once been stained, but that had been long ago. Mallard knocked. Ganderson waited behind him.

The woman who got up and approached from one of the two desks in the room on the other side of the door was fortyish and attractive, in Mallard's opinion, if slightly on the heavy side, which he did not mind at all. What he noticed was her hair, which was long, dark, and smoothly flowing. He also noticed her eyes, which were green and warm. She wore a smart orange blouse, an auburn skirt, and shoes with low heels. Her makeup was modest and tasteful. Behind her, at a second desk, was another woman, who appeared to be younger, smaller, and slimmer, with intense, nearly black eyes and curly brown hair that nested about her head.

"Yes?" The first woman waited on the other side of the door, next to which was a manilla card with red script that read "W.A.R.—Women at Risk." Under that, in smaller, black italics were the words *Counseling and Support*.

Mallard held up his badge, as did Ganderson.

The woman looked surprised. "What's this about?"

Mallard said, "May we come in, ma'am?"

The woman opened the door but didn't move. Ganderson and Mallard waited until she said, "Oh" and stepped back, then turned and went to the far side of the room, where a dozen folding chairs were stacked upright against a wall. She retrieved a chair and carried it to her desk. Mallard stepped to the stacked chairs.

"May I, ma'am?"

The woman smiled slightly and nodded.

While Mallard retrieved a second chair, the smaller, younger woman at the other desk watched. At a glance from the first woman, she rose, slid her chair to a spot beside her colleague's desk, and sat.

At one end of the room was a window that looked out over Beach City's business district. At the other were two easels that held posters describing types and effects of misogynistic abuse.

Mallard sat; Ganderson stood behind his chair. He had taken a small pad and a pen from inside his jacket pocket and was poised to begin writing.

"Would you tell us your name, ma'am?" Mallard asked.

The woman looked embarrassed. "Celia Worly, and this is…"

The other woman rose. "Lillian Walsh. Women at Risk is run under my auspices. I'm a social worker specializing in, well, women at risk."

"What exactly does that mean—women at risk?" Mallard asked as Ganderson took notes.

"Good question. It means different things to different women," Walsh answered. "We have women whose husbands are violent."

A loud knock at the door startled the officers, who had not heard anyone approach. The women appeared nonplussed by the tall, broad young man who looked blankly at them. His approach had been silent. In his hand was a large, white, nearly empty cup of a soft drink with a straw through its lid, such as one might purchase at a fast food restaurant.

"This is William," Lillian explained. "He helps out on a volunteer basis. We appreciate William." This last she said slowly, and obviously for William's benefit.

"Does William have a last name?" Ganderson asked, looking up at the young man and noting his size and weight.

William put up his hand. "My name is William Chase," he enunciated, "and I am twenty-seven years old. My birthday is in August. On August tenth, I will be twenty-eight."

"Please come in and sit down in the back, William, and wait until we're finished," Lillian said, then turned back to the detectives while William did as he'd been asked.

"Do you refer the women with violent husbands to the police?" Ganderson wanted to know. Mallard was still looking at William.

"Well, yes, but our primary function—our goal—is to offer them a safe space and some counseling—and to find a way to end the violence. We also give them tools for the future. So many women feel trapped by the men in their lives—and not just by husbands. Bosses, fathers, brothers, sons… If they want to bring the police in, the violence might get worse until they change their minds. Don't you see women who, when it comes to actually pressing charges against their violent husbands or boyfriends, change their minds?"

Mallard nodded. "Very often."

"Those women," Lillian Walsh said, "are captives."

From the back of the room, where he had taken a seat, William sipped his soda, which made a noisy slurping sound once the cup was empty.

Chapter 12

Celia Worly continued, "We have many women who, while not on the receiving end of violence, are abused at their jobs. Their bosses decide it's okay to touch them inappropriately—to pat them on the butt, touch their shoulders or arms…"

"Why don't they ask them to stop?" Ganderson wanted to know. Mallard looked at him and sighed.

"They often do," Worly answered. "But it's not so simple. They need their jobs. Their bosses are in positions of power. The women work hard and deserve promotions as much as anyone else, and speaking up about inappropriate behavior can undermine their careers, which is wrong."

Ganderson looked toward the window. "Which is life."

Mallard noticed a little smile on Lillian Walsh's lips as she looked at Ganderson.

"We're here because one of your patrons—"

"Clients," Walsh corrected.

"Clients—has been murdered."

Worly's hand went to her mouth; the only sign Walsh had heard was a clenching of her jaw. Her expression remained stoic.

"Lee—or Leonard—Travers."

Worly gave a little cry. "Lee?"

"No!" Walsh was shaking her head, holding up a "stop sign" hand.

"Tell us about her," Mallard requested gently.

"There are privacy issues. HIPAA issues," Walsh protested.

"For a dead person? This is a murder investigation," Ganderson growled.

"I'm not so sure about that," said Lillian Walsh stiffly.

"You don't think she was murdered?" Ganderson asked, confused.

"I'm not so sure a dead person doesn't have a right to privacy."

Ganderson shrugged, and no one spoke for a moment. When someone did, it was Celia Worly, who was trying not to cry. She had taken a few tissues from a packet on her desk and was dabbing at her eyes as she spoke.

"When Lee came to us, she was in high school and was sullen and obsessed with death." She shook her head. "This is so ironic."

"What's ironic, ma'am?" Mallard asked.

"She was beginning to learn to love life here," Worly said. "And now she's gone."

"Did she have any enemies—anyone who might have wanted to harm her?" Mallard asked.

Worly and Walsh looked at one another. Both shook their heads.

"She was sweet and gentle and kind," Worly explained, "though a bit introverted. She was having a hard time with the emotions brought out by the hormones."

"Hormones?"

"For transitioning," Worly went on. "She was a woman born in a man's body. She'd been taking hormones to inhibit testosterone and bring out—"

"The woman in her," Walsh finished.

Mallard had leaned toward Ganderson who raised an eyebrow. "Er, ah, HIPAA protection does survive death, Paul."

Ganderson looked annoyed and waved him away.

"When she came here, she was morbid, a bit goth and obsessed with death imagery," Worly confided, shaking her head with a rueful smile, "but she didn't really want to die."

"She loved to play soccer," Walsh added, "and was a good student, who excelled in history but did well in all her studies."

"She aspired to be a teacher," Worly added, "a high school history teacher, possibly a history professor. She was working with the guidance department toward applying to colleges—primarily state universities because they are affordable and the cost is so high elsewhere."

"The cost of transitioning was an issue," Walsh explained. "It isn't covered by insurance. Hence the hormones."

"Did she connect with other teens who wanted to…transition?" Mallard asked.

Lillian Walsh looked at Mallard for a long moment, thinking. "We have no other teens in her situation, but I believe that Lee participated in online forums for trans teens, which is how she found out about transitioning."

Her colleague nodded, and added, "I think that's also how she learned about us."

"Who were her friends?" Ganderson wanted to know.

The two women exchanged a look. "She mostly kept to herself here," Walsh answered. "You could try at the group home she lived in."

Walsh looked at Worly as though she had something to add but said nothing.

"Do you have adult clients in similar situations?" Ganderson asked.

"Similar—?" Walsh began.

"Transsexuals," Ganderson said.

"The appropriate term," Worly explained, "is transgender."

"I stand corrected," Ganderson said, looking pointedly toward the window.

"Giving out such information about clients—living clients," Walsh protested, "is highly irregular!"

"Not during a murder investigation." Ganderson looked steadily at her. Mallard looked away.

"Don't you need a warrant?"

"Not if you offer us information voluntarily," Mallard said.

The two women again exchanged glances.

"Lee's situation," Worly began, "is, was, unique. We don't have many clients like her."

"Many, or any?" Ganderson quickly asked.

Mallard looked at his partner, then at each of the women before asking, "What about Shelly Borzer—also known as Steven Berger?"

• • •

Sarah Turner was sitting next to her bedroom window, patiently attempting to nurse Livvie, as she and C3 called Olivia, whose response was on-again, off-again willingness—like someone who was sitting in their living room, daydreaming and occasionally sipping from a drink. Sarah was a bit frustrated but doing her best.

On a small, round glass table facing the window were a laptop, an iPad, and two cellphones. Sarah was singing softly and rocking, which had the opposite of her intended effect, lulling her daughter to sleep. But that was okay.

"Hush, Livvie darling, don't say a word. Mama's gonna get you a hummingbird…" Her phone whistled softly, her latest work-related ringtone. She looked, saw who it was, and answered.

"Chronicle."

"Sarah?"

"Lieutenant."

"How's the baby?"

"She's right here. All things considered, pretty good. She says 'hi.'"

Lieutenant Trask chuckled. "I have news. We had a murder night before last."

Once Sarah had the pertinent information, she thanked the lieutenant, ended the call, and wrote the press release. She then sent the release to Lemieux, who would post it on *The Chronicle*'s website and pass it along to Esther, who would post it to social media. She then covered her breast with the flap of her blouse and went back to singing to Livvie, who was fast asleep.

Twenty minutes later, her phone whistled again. She looked at the ID, took a deep breath, let it out, and answered the phone.

"Hi, Christine."

"You know what I'm calling about."

"Why don't you tell me?"

"We have beach season coming up, and we expect it to be a good one, especially as we emerge from this COVID situation."

"I'm with you there. We're already running summer fashion ad specials and any info the city gives us about events."

"Exactly. So is it in everyone's best interest for *The Chronicle* to put out these sensationalist releases and tweets?"

"Not if that's what they were, but that's not what we do."

"Have you read your release about this murder?"

"I wrote it."

"So wouldn't you say 'grisly' is a sensationalist word? A murder occurred. It has to be reported. I get that. But why scare potential business away from the city?"

"Christine. I—we are doing no such thing. This person had, according to police, been shot with a machine gun, which tore up the middle part of her body. The resulting injury was fatal…and definitely grisly."

"Grisly is a value judgment."

"I suppose, but how 'bout I get a hold of the image and send it to you and we can discuss?"

"Sarah, I'm only asking—"

"That we tailor the news to the mayor's preference. That we soft-pedal the truth."

Sarah could hear the mayor and her likely future mother-in-law breathing on the other end of the line.

"I only ask that you give it some thought."

"I'll do that, Ms. Mayor."

"Aw, you know I hate that."

"I do." Sarah smiled to herself.

"How's Livvie?"

"She's fine. She's asking for you."

Christine laughed. "Give her a kiss for me."

No sooner had Sarah ended the call and closed her eyes to nap with her daughter, when her phone rang again—this time with a line from a Grateful Dead song called "Mr. Charlie."

She summoned up a cheerful tone and took the call. "Charlie!"

"How's my little girl?"

"I'm fine."

"I mean my sweet granddaughter, though I'm glad you're well."

"We're both fine. I take it you don't like the press release?"

"Sarah, my concern is our coming beach season, and the vibrance of our community."

"Not its safety?"

"Of course its safety! Don't twist what I'm saying. I have clients who own boutiques. I run a co-op tourism advertising campaign…"

"And I run a newspaper."

"Well, it's online…"

"You know what I mean. Don't twist *my* words. I have to report the news, and I have to sell advertising, some of which is for your clients and their products. Why don't you call those clients and ask if it's okay for their ads to run near a story about a local murder, a story that will draw thousands of consumers' eyes, which sell products!"

Charlie Bernelli Jr. sighed. "Just making my feelings known to my future daughter-in-law, who happens to be captain of the local journalism industry."

Sarah laughed. "Such that it is." After ending the call, she dialed Dora, whom she knew would appreciate learning about the murder of young Lee Travers, and the information that came along with it.

• • •

The garden apartment complex was small and was a block from the beach. A u-shaped courtyard sported a sign that read Beach Gardens, which was the name of the complex. The building was also u-shaped and followed the outer contours of the courtyard. Amber brick facing on the front was bordered by darker red-brown brick along the edges and sides of the building. The apartments were all part of the same structure, with doors about twelve feet apart on both stories. Apartment 2E was on the second story, on the right side.

Ganderson knocked.

A dog could be heard barking, followed by a male voice calling, "Be right there!" The man who opened the door several inches was in his late

30s, had long brown hair, friendly deep-set brown eyes and wildly bushy eyebrows. "Detectives?" He held the door open with one hand, while holding back an eager golden retriever by the collar with the other. The two detectives filed past and entered the apartment. The man let go of the dog, which immediately began leaping up on the detectives' legs.

"Lady. Down!" The dog tempered her enthusiasm slightly, allowing the detectives to sit next to one another on a walnut-colored sofa. The man sat in a wine-colored upholstered chair.

Ganderson took out his notepad, which Mallard waved away, as he took out an audio recorder.

"Mind?" Mallard asked. The man shrugged.

"Let's start with your name," Ganderson began.

"Lowell Vains," the man replied.

"Spell that, please."

Vains obliged.

"Please tell us what you saw that led you to reach out to us," Mallard suggested.

"So I was walking Lady two mornings ago, and all I knew was she was barking way too much for six a.m."

"Seven a.m., sir."

"Huh?"

"You found the body at seven, sir—or so you told us when you called—and I believe this was three mornings ago."

"Really?" Vains scratched the top of his head for a moment, then nodded. The two officers looked at one another.

Vains continued. "Well, I'd only had my first of what're usually five cups of coffee, so it might as well have been three a.m. last month, far as I was concerned." He sat back, remembering. "Annnyyyway, all I saw was a hand. And this old girl"—he tugged on his dog's collar—"was barking like crazy—going nuts. When I saw the hand, I turned right around and came back in and called you guys. I don't have a cell phone you know. Can't abide the things. Always knew they'd be trouble, and I was right, wasn't I?"

Mallard nodded.

"Let me ask you something," Vains said. "What took you so long?"

Mallard switched off his recorder. "What do you mean, sir?" But he knew what Vains meant.

"I called three days ago."

Mallard could feel Ganderson looking at him; they both knew the answer. Trask had made sure the information was lost in the shuffle. Instead of responding, he turned for the door. "Thank you for your time, Mr. Vains."

Chapter 13

Dora and Missy sat in the back room of Geller investigations. Their chairs were pulled together at what they called the "guest desk," since it was the smaller of the room's two desks. The primary desk belonged to Adam Geller, who was rarely in the office, since he was so often out with clients or surveilling wayward husbands or disability cheats—the foundational pillars of the business. Investigating crimes was a recent addition, as were Dora and Missy who, as long as their clients paid their bills and as long as the two women remained part-time, were welcome to ply this new—for Geller Investigations—trade. Adam was beginning to find these cases more interesting than the foundational cases, though he might not freely admit it. Who wasn't fascinated by murder, and the various lurid contributing motives and means?

Today was a rare day he was at the office, winding up two cases, filling out forms that Thelma would later turn into invoices. His presence at the primary desk, his own, had displaced his two nascent investigators to the "guest desk."

"Why must a person's gender identification necessarily be a cause of their being the victim of a crime?" Missy wanted to know. "I'm sick of people assuming that because a person is gay, lesbian, or transgender, and happens to be the victim of a crime, that the crime was committed because of that fact."

"Who said that?" Thelma demanded. "You're being paranoid." Her braying voice carried such volume that she might as well have been yelling.

"*You* said that," Dora said. Missy was too diffident to engage directly with the always-aggressive Thelma.

"I never did!" Thelma cried, sounding as if she were right there in the room, despite being on the other side of a wall. Dora heard heavy footsteps, turned and saw that the fireplug of an office manager, ramrod straight with forever-brown hair rising Bride of Frankenstein-like, straight up from the side of her head, was in the doorway, leaning heavily against the door stop.

Dora ignored her and turned back to Missy. "I agree. These women have interesting, if challenging, lives. Some take hormones, some don't. Some have operations—medical transitions. Some are, as the name of the place suggests, simply women at risk—nothing to do with gender identification or preference."

"Exactly," Missy agreed. "And women are often taken advantage of, by men, by other women—"

"Usually by men," Thelma interjected.

"Agreed," Dora said. "And if they resist…" she began.

"Some bum tries to teach 'em a lesson," Thelma said evenly, in a voice that could be heard on the sidewalk.

"And nowadays," Missy added, "that might mean with a gun."

"In this case, an AR-15 automatic rifle," Dora clarified. "But what would be the circumstances around that?"

"I'm only saying," Missy said, returning to her original point, "that the fact that this kid, this Lee, happened to be a biological male who was living as a female—and maybe considered himself—herself, one, could be entirely beside the point."

"So, Miss." Dora looked at her partner. "Does all this info we have about Lee mean her death is completely unrelated to our investigation for Sawyer, into Shelly Borzer's disappearance?"

"I didn't say that," Missy answered. "On one hand, what are the odds—two trans women. One murdered, the other missing. On the other hand, think of what Lorne told us the other night. His brother—now sister—is due to inherit and goes missing, which would leave Lorne, you would think, as the sole heir." She paused. "Of course, you could also say that the fact that he's looking for his brother because they share an inheritance is a good thing—perhaps even a noble thing. They might not be able to execute the will without the two brothers being present."

"Unlikely," said Adam, who had looked up from his computer, interested in the conversation. "Lorne could receive his share of the inheritance while efforts remain ongoing to find the brother—what was his name?"

"Steven, originally," Dora said. "Now it's Shelly." She turned back to Missy. "So we agree, Miss, that maybe Lorne did something to Shelly, so as to keep the whole inheritance?"

"But why would he go looking for her? Why go to the cops to report her as a missing person? Wouldn't that jeopardize his plan?"

"Criminals love returning to the scenes of their crimes," Adam explained. "That's why arsonists watch the fires they set."

Missy looked curious. "So you think he went to the cops so he could follow the investigation into the murder he committed?"

Dora said, "And maybe stay a step ahead."

"Or maybe," Missy mused, "Shelly's afraid of Lorne. Maybe some of what you're suggesting is true, and maybe the inheritance has left her vulnerable. Maybe she's on the run."

Thelma nodded and pointed a firm finger at Dora. "That's what happened, one way or another. When money's involved, people—especially men—are capable of anything! Trust me!"

Dora dialed the office phone; she would have used hers, but she wanted to do things by the book—to make Adam happy and to keep Thelma, who was vehemently obsessive, off her back.

The phone was answered by a pleasant woman's voice. "Women at Risk—Celia Worly."

"Celia, this is Dora Ellison. I'm a private investigator at Geller Investigations here in Beach City."

"Hi. Yes, I've seen your sign."

"I'm wondering if you could tell me about someone who may have been a client or a participant there."

"Client would be the right word. Let me transfer you to Lillian Walsh. This is really her business."

Dora waited.

"Lillian Walsh."

Dora explained her reason for calling.

"Look," said Lillian, whose tone was far firmer than Celia Worly's, "I appreciate that, like us, you want to keep women safe. I really do, but the police pressured me to talk about our clients by explaining that theirs was a murder investigation, which I understand. There's very little I won't do for women's safety, given that there's very little others won't do to jeopardize it."

"Can you tell me if Shelly Borzer is a client?"

"I cannot."

"Even if her life's in danger?"

"Can you demonstrate to me that it is? Sounds like you've been hired to look for her. By the way, who hired you?"

"I really cannot divulge—"

"See? We both mean well, but we can't share all our information, and with good reason. We can't be open books, because we both have people to protect."

Dora thought about this. The woman had a point. "Can you tell me if a woman such as Shelly might have come to your organization?"

"What does that mean—a woman such as Shelly?"

"I mean a woman who'd been born a man."

"I can only say that our charter, our purpose, is to help protect and serve women who are at risk."

When their call ended, Dora saw that Adam was looking at her.

"These women—trans women—" he began.

"Yes?"

"Do they take hormones—female hormones?"

"I researched it a bit over the last few days," Missy responded. "They sometimes do—chemicals to enhance female qualities, along with androgen-blocking, testosterone-blocking hormones."

"That must be difficult for them," Adam observed.

"It might be, at least for some," Missy responded. "Why do you bring it up?"

"Because I've been taking ADT—Androgen Deprivation Therapy—for several weeks now."

"You have? Why?" Missy asked.

Adam paused, looking first at Missy, then Dora. "Prostate cancer."

Missy gasped; Dora put a hand to her chest. Still in the doorway, Thelma was shaking her head, her palm shading her eyes. When she looked up at her boss, her eyes were hard. "Is telling that to these…these children going to help any? You need to focus on other things, not your own troubles." Muttering, she turned and disappeared into the front of the office.

Chapter 14

The group sat in the bare room at the Beach City police station that was usually reserved for interviewing suspects and perps. Ganderson and Mallard had resisted Lillian Walsh's efforts to hold the meeting on her turf, at the W.A.R. offices or the schoolroom in which they held their meetings. The detectives had acceded to Walsh's insistence on being present for the meeting, and on having the clients who had agreed to the meeting be present *en masse.*

In addition to the group of W.A.R. clients, Lynn and Marty Travers, the victim's parents, were present. They were short and slight, like Lee, with similar pale complexions, sandy colored hair, and diffident dispositions.

"Er, eh, let me start by making clear to everyone," Mallard began, frowning and smoothing his blue paisley silk tie and absently stroking his diamond stud tie clip, "we're not here to antagonize anyone." He looked at Lillian in a way Dora knew was supposed to convey comfort and assurance, but which she could see instead engendered some degree of resistance. "We only want the truth, and to find justice for Lee."

Lee and Marty Travers looked at one another, nodding soberly.

"What can you tell us about Lee?" Ganderson asked, looking first at Lillian Walsh and then at Mr. and Mrs. Travers, all of whom looked at one another before Lillian began.

"Lee came to us about a year and a half ago. We have always been about women's safety, and when Lee came to us, we'd already had several women here of similar…" Her voice trailed off.

"These are women we're talking about," Lynn Travers interjected, "and you serve women." Her husband lay a gentle hand on her upper arm. She pressed her lips together and covered his hand with hers.

Walsh nodded. "Exactly. Lee came here because she was uncomfortable, insecure, and frightened."

"Of what?" Mallard asked.

"Of growing up," Marty Travers answered.

"Of being herself," Lynn Travers added.

"In a very real sense," Lillian Walsh reckoned, "Lee was like many of the women who come here." She looked around the room. "Would anyone care to mention why they came to W.A.R. in the first place?"

A cinnamon-colored woman with light brown hair that fell to her neck shyly raised her hand. "My name's Keisha—do I have to give my last—"

"No," Lillian said.

"My husband," Keisha said, "is a successful businessman—a Wall Street guy, and we do well." She hesitated. "Well, he does well. I can hear him in my mind, correcting me."

"Go on," Ganderson said.

"I found out he had—something on the side—some*one* on the side— and I was angry about that." Her eyes teared up. "And when I asked him about that, he—he hit me."

"You were afraid to come to us?" Ganderson asked softly.

Keisha didn't look at him. She was looking at a burly woman on the opposite side of the circle.

"I don't make it a practice to talk to cops," the woman said. "My name's Barb Skolnick—I don't care about giving my last name—and I own the pool hall in town. I don't have much to say except my mother was a vicious bitch—my father was long gone, so I guess she had her reasons. He scared the shit out of me before he left. Anyway, I came here to get some self-confidence. And I've got to say"—she looked gratefully at Lillian—"I've got some. Ain't no man fuckin' with me now. I'm my mother's daughter now!" She looked at Ganderson. "Cops neither!"

Ganderson smiled.

"What about Shelly Borzer?" Mallard asked.

"We've been over this," Walsh replied. "While someone like the woman you're talking about might come to us, you don't see her in the room, so she would not have been someone you've been given permission to talk to under our auspices. Whether or not she ever came to us or is currently a client, I couldn't say."

"Oh, for God's sake," Mallard complained, shaking his head.

"I'm sticking to our agreement," Lillian Walsh insisted. "Sterling? Do you have anything to add?"

Sterling, who was about thirty, androgynous, with short dark hair, luminous blue eyes, and a wry half smile, shrugged. "No, I don't really have much to say. Women at Risk helps me to feel safe. No one bothers me there, and I mostly just listen." Sterling paused, then added, "I don't identify as any particular gender. I identify as me, and that's it. I don't feel the need to take chemicals to look or feel some way, or to connect to some gender. That's not important to me—so hormones, or surgery—no thanks. Life's too short. I just want to enjoy it."

"What do you do for a living?" Ganderson asked.

"No comment," Sterling answered with a smile.

"I'd like to add something." It was Marty Travers. "Something that concerned my wife and me as Leonard was growing up. He was con-fused about who he was. I'm sure you can understand that. We're still a bit confused. Leonard read. He listened to podcasts. And—I don't know if this was right or not, but I wanted to shield him from pain." He paused to compose himself. "All this focus on trans this and trans that, and all the reading he did going over it all, over and over—" He began to cry. "I just wanted my son to feel like he was a kid—for him, or her, to *be* a kid, at least for a while. I kind of wish he could have focused on all of this when he…she was a little older."

Missy had folded her hands in her lap. She looked down at them. "We talk about this at the library. There are parents locally who are say-ing similar things, and who want us to keep certain books—books with certain topics—out of the hands of kids, for similar reasons. To keep them away until they're older. Of course if they have such issues them-selves, they may not have the luxury of waiting."

"Exactly," said Sterling.

Marty and Lynn Travers had bent their heads together until they were touching.

"Women," Lillian emphasized, "need to be able to be themselves. To be the women they are. And to be safe."

Mallard addressed the room. "Have any of you been made to feel unsafe?"

Every hand in the room went up.

Lillian smiled slightly at the detective. "Part and parcel of our gender."

"Let me rephrase for my partner," Ganderson said. "Have any of you been made to feel as though there might be a coordinated, direct threat to your lives on any particular recent days? That what happened to Lee—or to anyone else—might be part of a plot or threat stemming from some individual or group and targeting you or anybody here in particular?"

No hands went up.

• • •

Lieutenant Trask was standing in front of the two detectives' desks. "Just had a call from Celia Worly." She spoke to Mallard, ignoring Ganderson. "She said to tell you that Shelly Borzer was in fact a client." Trask smiled sweetly at Mallard for Ganderson's benefit, turned on her heels and walked away. Mallard chuckled.

Ganderson's office phone buzzed; he picked it up. "Ganderson."

"Sergeant Morse, sir. We've had a call from a man who says his dog found a woman's body off of Ocean Parkway, opposite Gugenheim Pond."

"Send forensics and a couple of cars and uniforms right away. Gerry and I will meet them there."

Ganderson hung up, took his coat from the back of his chair and nodded to his partner. "Woman's body. West of Gilgo."

They hurried out to their car and sped, lights and sirens, east through Beach City to the highways that led north and then east to Ocean Parkway, which was a long road through a narrow strip of land that separated the Atlantic Ocean from South Oyster Bay.

They arrived to find the scene secured with traffic cones and tape blocking off one lane of highway. A forensic tech had already arrived and was bent over what had once been a young woman—one who had apparently been mutilated by a high powered automatic rifle in much the same way as had Lee Travers. Unlike Lee Travers, this body was bloated and partially green, partially red—a combination of decomposition and accumulated gas. Foam had leaked from the nose and mouth and covered what was left of her face. Maggots and vermin had done their work and decimated much of what was left of her.

For the moment, the detectives had to stand a distance away, lest they disturb the scene. The tech, whose name was Sam and was in his mid-30s, stood up and walked a short way east, and showed the detectives the trail of still-broken vegetation through which the body had been dragged some days before.

The two detectives looked at the body as best they could from several vantage points, staying clear of the path from the road that Sam had shown them. Eventually, Mallard looked at his partner. "Shelly Borzer?"

"Too early to tell," Ganderson replied. "But I'm thinking so."

• • •

At day's end, before clocking off for the evening, the two detectives, who had been separately sifting information as it came in, compared notes.

"So I've got the Lee Travers info in front of me, whenever you're ready," Mallard said.

"Yup," said Ganderson, and he began to read what he'd been given by another tech who had been at the scene. "I've got an approximate date of the murder—that'd be the tenth. Five days ago."

"For Travers," Mallard said. "I've got the twelfth. Three days. And I've got a high-powered automatic rifle that tore up the groin and surrounding area."

"Same," said Ganderson. "And I've got bits of blue tarp and drag marks. Likely not the murder site."

"Check," said Mallard.

"Tactical desert-style bootprint. Size eleven or thereabouts."

"Well, same," said Mallard, "though it's one of many."

Ganderson continued. "Tire print from a truck, possibly a Ford, possibly an F-150."

Mallard looked at his computer screen. "No tire print here, but I do have a possible sighting, from one of the apartments across the street. Guy in a wheelchair who's always by his window said he saw someone—a guy—carrying something big over his shoulder. From the bed of a pickup that might have been a dark-colored F-150 to the beach."

Ganderson grunted.

"And a hock of dried, expectorated phlegm." Mallard grinned. "Killer with asthma."

Ganderson smiled back. "Thanks for the DNA, asshole."

Mallard looked at his screen, then at his partner. "What we need is a murder scene and some spent shells."

Ganderson pursed his lips and scratched the back of his head. "Well, if today was who we think it was, maybe we ought to look at the routes Shelly Borzer a.k.a. Steven Berger and Lee Travers typically took home from Women at Risk."

• • •

Late that afternoon, Dora and Missy walked along the beach hand in hand, watching Freedom and Comfort run in and out of the surf—Freedom in great leaping bounds and Comfort in tiny, rapid steps that were so fast that he essentially ran in place for a moment before going anywhere. They usually waited until just before sunset to take their beach walks, since dogs were technically not allowed on the beach. They also loved the cooler temperatures in the evening, and, of course, the sunsets.

The dogs returned to their sides; Freedom walked easily along, brushing now and then against Dora's thigh, letting her know that she was there and both offering and gaining protection. Comfort pranced joyously alongside Freedom, nipping at her heels when she seemed to stray from their owners' chosen path.

They walked west over two beaches, which were divided by jetties that aligned with the streets that ended at each beach. The sun slid silently toward the glittering water, with the sky overhead glowing scarlet, blending to violet, purple, and darkening blue.

Dora felt her phone vibrate, took it out, and looked at it. Missy looked at her, but Dora shook her head. "Won't be able to hear." So they walked north, away from the surf, until they reached the street, where Dora listened to the message.

When she was finished, she offered a partial explanation. "Let's bring the dogs back to my place. They'll be okay for a bit. We need to go to Rudy's."

"Was that Rudy?" Missy asked.

Dora shook her head. "You'll see" was her only answer.

Twenty minutes later, they walked through the door at Rudy's Bar and were warmly greeted by the enormous owner, Rudy Raines, who, along with his wife, the councilwoman Agatha Raines, were good friends. Rudy pointed them toward a table where an extremely young woman with luxuriously long blonde hair waited patiently.

"Hi. Willa Spencer."

"Of course," Dora said, as she and Missy sat down. "I remember."

"I have a couple of things that might be helpful with finding out what happened to Shelly."

"Go ahead," Dora encouraged.

"So Shelly and I used to come here sometimes after work and, well, about a month or so ago, we were here, and some guy was bothering us." Willa stopped talking suddenly and looked uncertainly at Dora and Missy.

At the next table, a group of men were drinking beer and ridiculing one another while eyeing three women standing at the bar whose backs were to them. It occurred to Dora that the attention from this group of men may have been unwanted. She thought about speaking up. Then one of the women turned and stared back at the men, leaning back with her elbows on the bar, her chest thrust forward.

"Hey," said one of the men.

"Hey yourself," the woman responded flirtatiously.

Dora realized that the interaction she was watching was probably a consensual two-way street.

"The secretary at our company," one of the men was saying to the others, "basically thinks she runs the place."

The woman at the bar heard him. "She probably does," she said, grinning. "Where would you be without her?"

"It's okay," Missy said to Willa. "No one's going to know you talked to us."

"What about the police—I mean, if it's something they should know?"

"Then you should tell them," Dora said; she didn't want to frighten the girl off, but neither did she want to mislead her.

"Well, okay. So Shelly told this guy who was bothering us to fuck off. This happened here. And he wouldn't—he just wouldn't. He was an A-hole, you know?" She grinned and giggled a little bit. "So Shelly called him over, and when the guy asked, 'What do you want?' Shelly said, 'It's not what I want, it's what you deserve' and kicked him right in the privates." She paused and stifled a laugh. "Shelly was ballsy like that. Well, the guy spread the word that he had Shelly's plates and was going to find her and kill her, but no one took him seriously. And now…" Willa bit her lip. "But I remembered it, so…"

"Thank you, Willa," Dora said. "You said you had a couple of things."

"The other thing is something I remembered she told me. Before Shelly was a colorist, she worked at a bank. And she used to help these criminals—real wise guys—launder money. I don't know exactly what she did, but one of those wise guys was the son of a real, I mean real wise guy. She used to talk about the kid—he was a real knucklehead— but his father was a super-rich real estate guy who was a corporate big- wig and also a criminal who no longer got his hands dirty. He was rich enough to, you know…"

"So Shelly got her hands dirty for him," Dora filled in.

Willa nodded, her eyes wide.

Chapter 15

Once the remains from the Ocean Parkway site were positively identified as Shelly Borzer's using the BCPD's Rapid DNA machine, the detectives began painstakingly tracing both women's routes home from the school where W.A.R. held its meetings. They began with Lee Travers, who lived only a short distance away and who was not known to own a vehicle, though there was always a possibility that she'd been given a lift. Both detectives wore gloves and carried tweezers and evidence bags for the task.

"When do you want to call Lorne Berger back in?" Mallard asked.

Ganderson looked grim. "Not yet." He didn't elaborate.

"His motive is clear," Mallard mused, "but why use an AR-15?"

Ganderson answered right away. "So he wouldn't miss."

Mallard didn't look as if he was buying his partner's answer. "And why the sexual mutilation?"

"A statement about his brother's gender identification, maybe. I don't know. People are sometimes way crazier than they seem. How many times have we seen that?"

Mallard had to admit, Ganderson had him there.

"But why would he ask us to look for his brother if he knew his brother was now his sister?" Mallard wondered.

"To throw us off," Ganderson snapped. "The brother being the perp would explain how he got close enough to kill Shelly," Ganderson continued. "Strange car approaches on the street at night, lot of people would run. But not if it's your brother."

"Whom you haven't seen in years," Mallard added. "But what about Lee Travers?"

"Maybe he knew Lee Travers too, through Shelly."

Mallard saw that Ganderson was staring at him. "What?"

Ganderson said, "Tell me something. Why would you wear that fancy suit for dirty street work?"

"This old thing?" Mallard flourished a hand down his side, indicating his light blue three piece suit. "This is my down and dirty, athletic stretch fit ensemble. If it was five hundred bucks, it was a lot."

"There it is again," Ganderson pointed out. "People are crazier than they appear."

The five-block walk was slow going, as the pair stopped to examine anything at all that might indicate a crime had taken place.

Two blocks later, Ganderson stood up straight and flexed his back, shaking his head at his partner. "You're a real piece of work, know that?"

Mallard grinned and grasped his jacket by the lapels, pulling it tighter around his shoulders. "Why, thanks, partner."

"That wasn't a compliment." Ganderson stooped to pick up a piece of material with his tweezers, rubbed it between his fingers, discarded it, stood up, and continued on.

"I know it." Mallard turned serious. "Someone's got to keep this team sane."

"Well, it ain't you." Ganderson shuffled away from the sidewalk and into the street as a young man with dark hair and a black beard walked by in the other direction with a gray pit bull on a short length of chain. Ever since a biting incident during an investigation two years earlier, Ganderson had been afraid of large dogs, especially pit bulls.

Mallard bent to take a close look at a maroon bit of something that had jumped out at him. He saw that it was a piece of candy wrapper and returned to his search. A few feet further on he paused again and squatted down. "Found something." He picked up a bit of blue material with his tweezers as Ganderson approached and took a look.

"Same blue tarp." Ganderson immediately began scouring the area. "Yup! Here's more—and looks like possible remnants of tissue and faint blood." He phoned the station, requesting a team to secure the site and more properly and completely collect the evidence.

"Where to next?" Mallard asked while they waited for the team to arrive.

"Shelly Borzer lived too far to walk. She either took an Uber or she drove."

"What about a bus?" Mallard asked.

Ganderson shrugged. "Could be. Let's start with Uber or car—see where we land."

Mallard nodded. "How 'bout we start with a car—the parking lot behind the school?"

"What I don't get," Ganderson said as they returned to their car, "is how these two murders would be connected. Lorne Berger's a perfect fit for Shelly—big time motive and opportunity. But Lee?"

"Let's not jump the gun—no pun intended. We don't know what we have until we know what we have."

• • •

The pair of detectives arrived at the school lot, parked along the side of the building and began walking concentric circles around the parking lot, their eyes on the ground, the walls of the building and the low concrete wall at the end of the lot opposite the building.

"Here!" Ganderson yelled after fifteen minutes, and Mallard jogged over. He pointed at a pattern of faded dark spots on the asphalt and the bottom of the concrete wall. "Blood spatter. And look at the gouges." Holes had been punched into the cement, and chunks had been torn away. "Automatic rifle," he said.

They examined the area further and found possible bits of bone, blood and flesh, along with a number of boot prints and tire tracks that might or might not have been relevant.

Mallard called for the forensics team and crime scene investigators to protect the scene and establish the proper chain of custody for any and all evidence.

• • •

Missy was surfing the Internet at the back of Geller Investigations while Dora stood in front of Thelma's desk.

"So how serious is his cancer?"

Thelma fixed Dora with a flat stare. "What cancer?"

"Don't play this stupid game," Dora said. "What cancer," she muttered. "Adam's prostate cancer."

"First off"—Thelma waggled a finger in the air—"talking to me like that will get you silence, permanently."

"Okay. I'm sorry. I apologize."

"Good start. And secondly, it's not my place to say. Boss wants you to know about his health, he'll tell you."

"But he already mentioned it when we were there. You were there, too."

Thelma grinned and shook her head. "Then you already know."

Dora went back to her seat in the back, thinking, *I just can't win.*

"I know what you're thinking," Thelma blared.

Dora didn't doubt it.

Missy surfed the Internet while Dora phoned the Rainbow Salon and waited. "Is Sawyer in?" she asked. "Dora Ellison," she responded, when asked who was calling.

"Sawyer speaking."

"Hi, Sawyer. I have a question. What was the name of the bank where Shelly worked before she came to you?" She waited while

Sawyer considered the question. "Terrific. Thanks!" She turned to Missy. "Northeast Federal Savings—or so she thinks."

Missy had found what she was looking for and made a note of it in her Google Doc.

"We heading over there?" Missy asked, but Dora was already up and heading for the door. Ten minutes later, they walked into the local branch of Northeast Federal and waited while the manager, who was in a partitioned cubby, finished with a customer.

Several minutes later, a honey-colored woman in her forties with shoulder-length black hair approached the two women with a smile. "Please come in." She waited while Dora and Missy sat.

Missy took out a card and handed it to the woman, whose gold name plate read Imara Varma in black letters. Varma's lips made a circle as though whistling. She nodded slowly.

"Private investigators? Is this treasury related? Are you investigating the bank?"

Missy shook her head. "We're investigating a murder."

Varma looked shocked. "A murder? At the bank?"

"Not at all. We are hoping to get a little bit of information about one of your customers."

Varma's eyes narrowed. "I see. Who would that be?"

"Actually, we're not sure."

"Well then, I don't see how I can—"

"He is or was a successful real estate developer in the area. Probably the most successful in the vicinity."

Varma blinked. "Well, even if I knew who that would be, I couldn't give you information as to whether or not a particular individual banked here. That is not allowed."

"With a warrant?" Dora wanted to know.

"You're not treasury, and you're not police. I would be surprised if you have a warrant. But if you had a warrant, or a court order—"

Dora sighed and shook her head.

"That's okay. Never mind." Missy smiled. "Thank you, Ms. Varma."

The woman smiled politely, and Missy rose to leave. Dora looked at her, then followed.

"What was that about?" Dora asked when they were in the car.

"Let's have a drink and discuss."

Dora glanced at Missy. "Rudy's?"

"Rudy's."

They sat down at one of the small, round tables in the front room of Rudy's bar. Dora waved to Rudy, but he was deep in conversation with two people at the back end of the bar. One was a tall, bald, ebony man in a close-fitting, forest green suit, lime green dress shirt and gold tie, tie clip and cuff links. His eyes were hidden behind dark sunglasses. Beneath and to either side of his nose was a perfectly groomed handlebar mustache. Next to him was a slighter, slender, androgynous person with a hard, powerful-yet-at-rest look—like a jungle cat—dressed in burgundy, Merino wool sweat pants, a matching shirt, belt, and fanny pack.

Dora approached, looking at Rudy. "'Scuse me, Rude. Can we get two—"

"We're talking right now." The jungle cat remained utterly still, yet seemed filled with gathered energy, and fixed a stare at Dora the way a cat is riveted to its prey.

Dora stopped, surprised but not angry. She looked at Rudy, who held up a finger.

"With you in a minute," he said *sotto voce* with two quick nods, indicating not to worry.

Several minutes later, Rudy arrived at their table, grinning and shaking his head.

"Who're those two?" Dora asked.

"Those are two of the baddest dudes I ever met. You do not want to know."

"Is the smaller one a man?"

Rudy huffed a breath. "The smaller one is by far the more dangerous of the two, and is neither a he nor a she, but a ze."

"A ze?" Missy's eyes rounded. "I never heard of a ze."

"Well, now you have. And if Skye wants to be called ze, then that's what I call zim. Trust me on that."

Dora was looking at Skye with interest. Skye stared right back.

"Did I piss Skye off just by coming over to talk to you?"

Rudy shook his head. "Take a lot more than that. You piss Skye off, you'll know about it."

"Huh," was all Dora said.

"Anyway, I explained to Skye that you two are good people—that you helped my family when we was in deep shit." Rudy smiled warmly.

"I explained that you're both family. Now—a beer and a glass of wine?" He nodded in the direction of his two friends at the end of the bar. "Ze's already paid."

Dora and Missy instinctively glanced toward the end of the bar; Rudy's two friends had lifted their glasses in greeting. Missy waved; Dora gave a thumbs-up. Once Rudy had gone, Dora turned to Missy, who was still glancing nervously at their new friends.

"So, Miss. You were saying?"

"Oh, right. Well, I'm pretty sure Avram Rivkin's the developer we were talking about. His son, the knucklehead Willa was referring to as having it in for Shelly, is Isaac Rivkin."

Dora held out her hands, palms up. "What, you read her mind?"

"No, I surfed the net. Before going to the bank, I looked up local real estate moguls with sons who're connected. Mr. Google's good with stuff like that, long as you know what to weed out, what to believe and not believe."

"Whoa!" Dora was impressed.

"Not only that, but I don't think Isaac Rivkin was involved in Shelly Borzer's death."

"Why not?"

"He's in the third year of a seventeen-year sentence for money laundering."

Dora nodded slowly. "Ah."

"And in my humble opinion, the other guy Willa talked about didn't do this either. That sounded to me like a petty grievance, like if someone looked at someone funny or cut someone off with their car. Pissed off at the moment, but to really kill someone? Possible, but I don't think so."

"The guy did threaten to kill Shelly."

"Maybe so, but there are threats and there are threats."

"Hmm," Dora said, eyeing Missy with newfound respect. "Aren't you the worldly one."

• • •

It was early evening, and Paul Ganderson was reading the report that had just been delivered to his desk. He looked across the desk at Mallard, who was arguing with his wife on the phone.

"Please hang up, Gerry."

Mallard held up a finger. "Er, ah, sweetheart—now, darling, there's no need for that. No, I am not irresponsible with my promises—Kay, love, I'm a police officer, in case you haven't noticed. That means my schedule is at the, ah, whims of, er, criminals. I am not being sarcastic; I'm telling you the truth. And isn't that what you always ask me to—yes, I know it's dinner time!"

Ganderson raised his voice. "Just tell her she's right already, and let's get back to work."

"Just a moment," Mallard said, into the phone. He turned to Ganderson. "Kay says hi and asks how your sore throat is feeling today."

Ganderson rolled his eyes and said, "Please thank her and tell her it's better, but we really have to get to work on this case."

Mallard listened as his wife spoke, then smiled and shook his head, looking at his partner. "She says of course, why didn't I say so?" He hung up. "Sheesh."

Ganderson looked steadily him. "That's what happily married sounds like?"

Mallard nodded sadly. "It is." Then he smiled. "What've you got?"

Ganderson held up the paper he'd been reading. "So the trace evidence we found in the street and in the lot do indeed indicate that these are the murder scenes of Lee Travers and Shelly Borzer, a.k.a. Steven Berger. Obviously, the relevant tie they shared was their involvement at Women at Risk, but who would be killing women who go to counseling centers?"

"Trans women, and it's a relevant tie—not *the* relevant tie. There may be others."

"True, and according to the M.E., one was a trans woman, the other was a man."

Mallard said, "Know what? If you're amenable, I have an idea." He pulled up a Women at Risk meeting schedule on his computer.

An hour and fifteen minutes later, the two detectives had split up and were waiting at the two exits of the school where Women at Risk held their meetings—Mallard at the front, Ganderson at the back.

Several minutes after the scheduled end to that evening's meeting, Barb Skolnick exited via the back door of the school. Ganderson had been waiting off to one side and approached her.

"Ms. Skolnick?"

The burly woman started and stared at Ganderson. "You're that cop!"

"Can we have a word?"

"Who's we?" she asked suspiciously.

Ganderson spoke into his phone. "Come on around back."

"What if I don't want to?" Skolnick asked, her tone belligerent.

"Then you don't have to. You're not in any trouble. This isn't about you. We're asking for your help. Your insight. That's all."

Walking quickly, Mallard came around the side of the building.

"I don't want to go to the station," Skolnick insisted. "Police stations give me the creeps."

"How 'bout we sit in the car?" Mallard asked, keeping his tone polite.

"Air conditioning? I'm having hot flashes."

"We'll blast it—how's that?"

"Well…" Skolnick hesitated. "If you sit in the back."

"That's fine," Mallard agreed.

Once settled in the detectives' car, with Mallard in the back and Skolnick in the front with Ganderson, the burly woman hesitated.

"I don't know about this."

"Paulie, see if you can turn the AC up higher," Mallard said from the back. Then he said to Skolnick, "I can see why you don't want to sit back here. Not a good time."

Skolnick laughed, despite herself—the throaty, phlegmy laugh of a smoker. "See what I'm sayin'?" she said.

"Look," Ganderson began patiently, "we only want to know if there was anyone in the group who might not like the two women who were killed."

"You mean trans women in general, or just those two?"

Ganderson shrugged. "Either."

Skolnick eyed a fit man in his mid 30s with dirty blond hair in a ponytail. "Nice ass," she said.

"So..?" Ganderson prodded.

"Gotta tell ya, I think trans women are kind of creepy. You don't know if they're comin' or goin.' Now, women I understand."

"Um," Ganderson said, trying to parse the woman's language.

"Well, there's a woman named Keisha who comes here and had some kind of grudge against Shelly. And you know what else? There's a crowd of women—what we used to call mean girls in school, you know? They're sort of a clique, and they judge people. And I know they don't like women like the two you're asking about."

Ganderson was squinting at Skolnick, and Mallard could see that his partner didn't believe her.

"What are their names?" Mallard asked.

"Darla, Reece, Keisha—who I just mentioned—and Winona. But the leader is Winona. They started off just like the rest of us—girls who had taken enough shit and weren't taking any more, or who were freaked out or, in some cases, addicted. Some were in the life, you know. Anyway, after a while, you could see that when Winona disagreed with someone, she would somehow get other women to disagree with that person, until they had this clique going. There would be this social pressure. Then when Shelly Borzer came, and Lee and a few other trans women, well, Winona didn't like them."

"Why?" Mallard asked.

Skolnick thought for a moment. "Because they were different. And they didn't respond to peer pressure the way the other women did. I mean, look, I'm no shrink, but it seems to me that they learned how to deal with others when they were kids. And when they were kids, they were boys, or part of boy groups—I'm assuming. I don't know. But anyway, Winona didn't like them. The clique shit didn't work on them."

"Huh," said Ganderson dubiously.

Skolnick held up a stubby finger. "You know who else? William. He's this creepy guy—not all there, you know? He helps out."

Ganderson said, "And he didn't like Lee Travers or Shelly Borzer?"

"Well, I didn't say that, but he's creepy, and a couple of slices short of a pie." She grimly pressed her lips together and nodded, emphasizing her point. "Oh, one more thing. Lee had this friend—a guy. He didn't come to W.A.R., but he was a close friend. Kind of a dweeb of a kid. They were close, but he'd hurt her somehow—like she was close with him, and he hurt her. She didn't let a lot of people in, and she did let him in, and somehow he burned her. Name was Doug."

Chapter 16

That night, Dora and Missy were walking on the beach when they were approached by muscular young man in a dark blue tank top who said, "I know you! You're that private eye, Dora Ellison!"

"Well," Dora answered politely, "Missy and I are a team."

"I know who you are," the man insisted. "And listen, I'm here to send a message. Stop looking into those murders."

"What murder are you referring to?" Dora could feel Missy go rigid beside her; she took Missy's hand and squeezed it.

His voice fell into a macho drawl. "You know what fuckin' murders—the ones connected to that women's group."

Dora sounded cheerful. "See? I knew you'd tell us. Look, I have a job to do. Why would I want to stop doing my job?"

"Because if you don't, you'll wish you did."

"Really? I don't think so."

"You're not listening." The man produced a knife.

Dora let go of Missy's hand and moved between her and the man. "How about you and your little knife go on home, and do your whittling or whatever, before you get hurt."

"I'm not going anywhere."

Dora sighed. "You don't understand. You'll lose your knife, and I guarantee I'll break at least two of your fingers."

"It's you who don't understand." Another man was a dozen yards away and walking toward them in the soft sand. He wore dark clothing and no shoes. One of his hands was raised in front of him and held what appeared to be a pistol. As he came closer, Dora saw that it was a SIG Sauer P365 subcompact semi-automatic, and he was too far away to charge, whether by dropping and rolling or drop stepping or running in a zig-zag pattern.

"Nathan," said the man with the gun, "stay off to that side while I walk them into the sea. Once we're done, we'll ride back up together."

Nathan looked unsure of himself. "We still split the money?"

The man sighed. "Yeah, Nathan. We still split the money."

"I have a better idea," said a third voice. Dora saw movement against the backdrop of a dune, but it was hard to tell given the dark night. The voice was familiar.

The second man had swiveled to point his gun in the direction of this third voice, then back again at Dora. He pivoted repeatedly, attempting to cover Dora as well as whomever the new voice belonged to.

"Here's what we're going to do," said the new voice. There was a muffled sound like the mewing of a kitten, and the man with the pistol quietly fell to the sand. Something dark was spreading over his forehead. Nathan's eyes were wide; he was rooted to the spot.

"There now, Nathan," said the third voice, and out of the shadows stepped Skye, the androgynous person who had been at Rudy's. Skye grinned at Dora. "Been keeping an eye on you. Rudy said you could handle yourself as well as anyone, but can't all use a helping hand now and then?"

"You're right about that." Dora gave a relieved smile.

All Missy could say was, "Ohhh!"

"See now, Nathan," Skye continued. "Now you could keep all the money—if there was any. But since you and your pal didn't do your job, I suspect there won't be. What you will have though is much more valuable." Skye paused. "Your life. So at this point, what I'd suggest is to go back wherever you came from, and tell whoever you work for to stay away from Dora, Missy and this whole damn town, or I'll come find them. How's that?"

"Sounds great to me," Nathan quickly agreed. "So I can go?"

"You not only can, you'd better."

As they watched Nathan hustle away from the beach, Dora took a deep breath. "Thank you, Skye."

"No need," Skye said, nudging the body with a toe, picking up the pistol and slipping it into a pocket; his own went into a holster in the small of his back. "Come on. Someone'll find this guy and call it in. Let's book to Rudy's. You're buying."

• • •

Mallard listened to the call that Lieutenant Trask had just put through to him. The caller's information was interesting and possibly relevant, but the caller, who sounded like a young woman, insisted on remaining anonymous. After ending the call, Mallard explained the situation to Ganderson, then called the Rainbow Salon.

"Sawyer Townsend please," he said.

"Sawyer's with a client right now," said the person who answered the phone. "Can you call back in an hour?"

"Tell her it's Beach City Police Detective Gerry Mallard, and it's important."

Moments later, Townsend came on the line. "Detective?"

"Can you tell me if you have a woman named Keisha working there?"

"Sure, Keisha Williams."

"We have reason to believe that she disliked Shelly Borzer. Can you confirm that?"

"Interesting that you'd ask. Yes, there was animosity between Keisha and Shelly. Keisha is one of the few people I can think of who didn't like Shelly, but it was a professional thing—jealousy because everyone loved Shelly—possibly more than they did Keisha, and that rankled Keisha."

"Why do you say it's interesting that I ask?"

"Because I gave this some thought after I read that Shelly's body had been found and identified. But Detective, whatever trouble there might have been between them was just jealousy—nothing on a par with what happened to our poor Shelly. In fact, we had a little memorial at the salon, and we dedicated a permanent chair in Shelly's memory, and Keisha spoke at the memorial, acknowledging her bad feelings and expressing regret."

"And you believe that she was being genuine?"

Townsend's words were heartfelt. "I do. I really do."

After ending the call, Mallard explained what Townsend had told him.

"You believe her?" Ganderson asked.

Mallard's expression was equivocal. "Don't know. Speaking at a memorial is pretty good cover, but murdering someone with an AR-15 over workplace jealousy is a stretch."

Ganderson wasn't convinced. "I've known some nasty jealous women in my time, and I wouldn't put anything past them."

"Maybe so," Mallard agreed, "but for now, let's chase down the solid stuff and leave the rumors and petty crap on the back burner."

• • •

"Nice place." Dean Clayburgh stood just inside the door next to Charlie Bernelli Jr., a plastic bag in his hand, admiring Charlie and Christine's apartment—the polished wood floors, the sunken circular sofa in the center of the room, the steel staircase winding upward to the second floor of the penthouse, the floor-to-ceiling windows that looked out over the ocean. He admired them all for a long moment, then spied the bar. "Ah," he said, and shuffled over that way, the moccasins he wore on his otherwise bare feet making swooshing sounds on the wood. He went right for the single malt.

Everyone else was there. Christine was in the kitchen, putting the finishing touches on the turkey and C3 and Sarah were in the living room listening to the Grateful Dead played softly over the stereo, while

Olivia was asleep in a carrier that doubled as a car seat on the floor at the couple's feet.

"Charlie?" Christine poked her head out of the kitchen, smiled at her husband, then paused, looked at Clayburgh, then back at Charlie for a long moment. "Would you please move some of the settings over and add another place at the table?"

"You don't want me to do that." Charlie was pouring himself a single malt—a double. "I have a guest here."

Christine said, "Wouldn't you like him to join us at the table?"

"Yes, but I'm entertaining. You're handling the household stuff at the moment. Maybe C3 can do it. Hey C—would you move another chair to the table for my guest?"

Christine said something unintelligible, then disappeared back into the kitchen while C3 moved the chair.

"I knew I'd be unexpected, so I brought a little something." Clayburgh put down his glass and began taking single portion bags of HelthE Snax from the plastic bag he'd brought and placing them on each of the plates on the dining room table. When he returned to his drink, he turned to Sarah and C3. "Can I fix you folks drinks?"

Sarah shook her head. "No thanks. I don't drink and C3's sober."

Clayburgh raised his eyebrows, nodded, then pointed his chin at the baby. "What about—?" He laughed, then joined Charlie Jr. at the windows.

Eventually, Christine emerged from the kitchen wearing a bright red apron and set a place for Clayburgh in front of the chair C3 had brought over, then announced, "Dinner's about to be served!" and returned to the kitchen.

The guests each found their places as Christine brought in plates of mashed potatoes and vegetables.

"Let me help," Sarah offered.

C3 laid a gentle hand on her shoulder. "No, let me." He went into the kitchen, where Christine kissed him on the cheek, and returned carrying the turkey. Christine then brought in a white serving dish of applesauce and a pitcher of sweet tea. C3 made a second trip for the gravy and yams.

Once everyone was sitting and Olivia was behind her parents in the carrier, Christine folded her hands. "Bless us, O Lord, and these Thy gifts, which we are about to receive from Thy bounty. Amen."

"Amen," the guests repeated, as Charlie passed the first plate of food to his wife.

As the food began cycling around the table, Clayburgh looked at Sarah. "So I understand you run the local newspaper."

Sarah nodded. "*The Chronicle*—it's an online weekly."

"So Charlie told me, and I happened to peruse the most recent issue earlier today. Very nice!"

"Thanks. I inherited it from the previous editor, who was also the founder. I worked for him for a year and a half, and when he…left, it fell into my lap."

"It's impressive that a young woman in your situation would be running a news source."

"Sarah works from home most of the time," C3 explained. "Much of the business is virtual."

"Do you work—C3, is it?"

C3 nodded. "I'm Charlie Bernelli the Third—everyone calls me C3. Yes, I do. I drive an Uber and am working toward getting back my job at a local counseling center."

"Getting back your job?"

Charlie quickly began to explain, "He just means—"

But C3 cut him off. "It's okay, Dad. I'm a recovering addict. I was a drug counselor but had a relapse. Now I'm working toward getting my position back, which I expect will happen soon."

Clayburgh shook his head. "Boy, you folks do talk about everything."

Christine smiled.

"So I happened to read in your paper, Sarah, about these two murders of what you call trans women."

"Murders of two women, yes," Sarah said.

"Well, like our hostess, I'm a churchgoer, and I can't understand why a person who is made by God to be a man would want to change what he was ordained to be."

Sarah gave him a hard look. "And I can't understand why folks who have their own business to attend to would want to poke their nose into other folks' business."

The plate of turkey had reached Christine, who set it down, stabbed a thigh that was still attached to a leg with her fork, and drove her knife down hard between the thigh and leg, slicing through the cartilage and separating the two. The knife passed through the bird's flesh and hit the plate below with a sharp clang.

Clayburgh didn't seem to notice. "I encourage you to try my HelthE Snax with dinner. They really do go perfectly with everything, and they're chock full of goodness."

• • •

Two days later, Ganderson and Mallard returned to the school where W.A.R. held its meetings. They had already made calls to both the group home where William Chase lived with a handful of other special needs adults with minimal supervision and maximum freedom, and to one Douglas Szerbo, who had befriended Lee Travers at the halfway house in which they had both lived.

"Well, it sounds as if he could handle the AR-15 in terms of physical strength," Mallard observed of Chase, "but he also sounds like an easy-going guy who loves his job."

Ganderson said, "Maybe he's got one of these invisible rage things going on."

"Maybe so," Mallard admitted. "But what would his motive be?"

"Who knows? Something hidden?" Ganderson suggested. "Something no one else would understand. He has a developmental disability. Maybe a misunderstood slight, or a mental illness issue."

"Well, having developmental disabilities doesn't mean the guy has mental illness. That could be true of anyone. But I'm not getting any sense of that—and I have the same feeling for opposite reasons for this Doug guy. Sounds a little flightier—"

"And a lot more intelligent," Ganderson added.

"But maybe not physically up to handling an automatic rifle." Mallard noted. "Maybe we go see both those guys."

Ganderson didn't answer directly. "I'll tell you who could handle an automatic rifle—Barbara Skolnick. She's a tough cookie who seems to resent all sorts of people."

"And she knew Shelly Borzer from two places—W.A.R. and the Rainbow Salon."

"Well," said Ganderson, "let's see what turns up here."

They waited separately outside the two school exits as they had with Barbara Skolick until a tall, willowy, pretty young woman with short sun-bleached blonde hair exited the front of the building.

"Winona Lofer?" Mallard asked.

The woman smiled easily and confidently. "Who wants to know?"

He held out his shield, then spoke into his phone. "Around front." He looked back at the woman. "My partner and I would like a word— would that be okay?"

Lofer gave him a mock serious glance. "You're not taking me down-town?"

"No, no. Nothing like that. Just a few minutes to chat."

"Do I need a lawyer?"

"Do you?" Mallard shrugged. "Up to you. But you're not being arrested or accused of anything." They began walking toward the back of the building, where they joined Ganderson in a corner of the lot.

Lofer looked around. "This feels like a drug deal," she said nervously. "Not that I have any knowledge of drug deals!"

The detectives laughed.

"So tell us your thoughts about Lee Travers, Shelly Borzer, and the other trans women at Women at Risk."

Lofer looked confused. "Well, I have no opinion of them as a group because they aren't a group—they're individuals. If you're asking what I think of trans women, you might as well ask what I think of women who wear blue. I don't think anything of them. They are who they are, which is none of my business."

"Okay," said Ganderson. "What about each of them individually?"

"Well, obviously I'm shocked and sad that anyone's been killed. I don't understand it. They seemed perfectly okay—not in any trouble that I could see or anything."

"Rumor has it you were not fond of either one of them," Mallard said.

"Rumor? I don't indulge in rumor—and I wouldn't think the police would, either. I would have thought you deal in facts, not rumor." She tilted her face upward, and when she looked at the detectives the effect was as though she were looking down on them.

"Our understanding is that you deal quite a lot in rumor," Mallard mused.

Lofer laughed. "Now *that's* a rumor!"

"What did you think of Lee Travers?" Mallard insisted.

"I didn't think of Lee Travers. Nor did I think of Shelly Borzer—not very much, really. Why would I?"

"We have had reports that you—"

"Yeah, that I didn't like them, which isn't true. I mean, they were okay. I have nothing against either of them, per se. Some people have weird ideas, not in general, but specific ideas I might or might not agree with. I'm a person who speaks her mind, and hey, if some people tend to agree with me, I like to think that has something to do with the quality of my ideas or my means of expression more than anything else—certainly more than my being bigoted."

"We never said you're bigoted."

"Didn't you?"

"Not us," Mallard said, shaking his head.

"So who said I didn't like trans people?"

"No one," said Mallard.

Lofer narrowed her eyes. "Then why are you here?"

"To see if you might know anyone who might have had anything against either Lee Travers or Shelly Borzer—perhaps both."

"Well, why didn't you say that?" She looked at Mallard, then at Ganderson. "Anyway, I don't."

• • •

When Ganderson and Mallard exited Chief Stalwell's office, neither was in any mood to talk. Being chewed out by the normally mild-mannered chief was bad enough, but to have Waycrest chiming in every minute or so, twisting the knife, was more than either detective wanted to have to deal with.

When they returned to their desks, Ganderson was furious, and Mallard was his own equivalent—mildly annoyed and devoid of his typically cheerful, lackadaisical demeanor.

Sweat stained the collar of Ganderson's shirt, and his neck was red-splotched and glistening. "Am I supposed to care what the mayor thinks about this case and how it might affect our beach season? What the hell do they think we're doing, if not investigating?"

"You're right, Paulie," Mallard nodded somberly. "And the president of the freakin' chamber of commerce! When you're right, you're right."

"Is the lack of evidence our fault?" Ganderson railed.

Mallard had taken out a $400 handkerchief and was mopping his forehead. "A bit of tarp, a tire, and boot print don't give us much to work with," he lamented.

"Everything else is he said, she said. Bullshit conflict!" Ganderson threw his hands in the air. "Rumor. No shells—so far, anyway. No witnesses—fuck's sake!"

"Let's go see that disabled guy who works at the women's center—William Chase," Ganderson said suddenly. "And you know what? Let's go see Doug Szerbo too. Which one do you want?"

• • •

Lillian Walsh had insisted on being present when Mallard interviewed William Chase, and she'd insisted that the interview take place at her office. The detectives did not have to agree, since Chase was an adult, but they wanted to maintain a cordial relationship with Walsh, since she was a gatekeeper to many people who knew the victims.

The three sat in a small circle of chairs in the center of the room.

"Do you understand why we're here, Mr. Chase?" Mallard asked.

"You're a police officer," the young man answered, smiling because he knew the answer to the question.

"That's right," Mallard said, smiling back. Lillian Walsh looked on with a stoic expression.

"I'm here to ask about the two women who died," Mallard continued.

Chase looked at Walsh, then back at the detective.

"He knows…what happened?" Mallard whispered to Walsh.

She nodded. "Go easy," she urged.

"William," Mallard said, "I need to ask you some questions about the women who were killed. May I do that?"

Chase nodded as tears sprang into his eyes.

"Were you friendly with Shelly Borzer and Lee Travers?"

Chase nodded. A tear trickled down one of his cheeks. "We were friends. I liked Shelly. I didn't know the other one."

"You didn't know Lee?"

Chase shook his head.

"Lee kept to herself," Walsh interjected.

"Did you ever argue with either Shelly or Lee?"

Chase shook his head. "They were nice. I didn't know Lee, but she seemed nice."

"William—do you know who killed either of them?"

Chase face contorted, and he began to cry.

"William?" Walsh prodded. "Please answer the detective."

Chase shook his head violently and began to wail.

Mallard asked, "Do you mean you don't know?"

"I don't know! I don't know! I don't know!" Chase was crying harder now.

"I think that's enough," Walsh said firmly.

• • •

Wally Peterson, the house supervisor, let Ganderson in and pointed him to Doug Szerbo's room, outside of which the detective now stood, knocking hard on the door and waiting. Loud metal-style rock and roll was emanating from the room, so after knocking once more, Ganderson opened the door.

Szerbo was lying on his bed wearing jeans, a T-shirt with the logo of a well-known heavy metal band, and no shoes or socks. His straight dark hair fell over his eyes, which were closed. He was playing invisible drums wildly, arms flailing, head jerking on each beat. Eventually he opened his eyes, saw Ganderson, and immediately shut off the music and scooted to the far side of the bed, his knees drawn up against his body.

"My name's Detective Paul Ganderson. I was hoping to ask you a few questions."

Szerbo didn't answer; his eyes were enormous and worried.

"I understand you were friendly with Lee Travers."

Still no answer.

"Well?"

A tiny nod.

"Please speak your answer."

"I was friends with Lee," the young man said.

"I also understand that Lee did something that hurt you—isn't that true? That there was a problem between you?"

Szerbo's eyes darted away—toward the blank wall to his left.

"Please answer the question, Doug."

Szerbo started to shake his head but caught himself. "No, it's not true."

Ganderson sighed. "So, right up until her death, everything was fine between you and Lee Travers—is that what you're telling me?"

This time Szerbo looked Ganderson in the eye. "Yes, sir," he said. "It is."

"That's not the information we have."

Anger flashed in Szerbo's eyes. "Well, your information's wrong." Hearing his own words and tone, Szerbo fearfully retreated into himself and refused to answer any more questions.

• • •

Missy was on the floor with her head on Freedom's back while Comfort's head lay in her own lap. Dora was sitting on the couch, focused on closing in on her puzzle's finish. The puzzle had been made from a photo of a summer night sky, awash in pinpoint stars floating in an inky background. The puzzle, which had been a birthday gift from Vanessa Burrell and her sons, for whom Dora often babysat, was particularly difficult because so much of it looked the same. Dora looked up from the puzzle, got up from the couch, went to Missy and the two dogs, bent over, and kissed Missy lightly on the lips.

"So, can we talk about moving in together?"

Missy opened her eyes. "Sure. But I'm—"

"Afraid that I'll get hurt?"

Missy nodded. "Well, that one of us will."

"I won't let that happen."

"Easy to say, and I know you mean it, but I'm…just afraid to rock the boat."

"We won't be together all that much more than we are now, and any risks would be mitigated by our being together. You'd be a good influence."

Missy laughed. "Nice try."

"So?" Dora pouted. "How 'bout it?"

"Give me a bit more time to think about it. I'm still kind of terrified of your violence."

"I'm working on it. Maybe you could help. I promise I'll keep at it, but when we're not together, I really miss you. And look, I know we work together, and not a lot of couples can manage that."

"That's another thing," Missy said. "Would work create a problem for us if we live together?"

"We wouldn't have to let it. Anyway, it's not a problem now. So…" Dora's phone rang. "Think about it." She picked up her phone from the coffee table next to the puzzle. "Hello?" She listened, then hung up. "That," she said, "was a young person named Sterling who goes to Women at Risk."

"I remember."

"Right. And Sterling says there's one woman there who deeply resents nonbinary people and trans women."

"Who would that be?"

"Lillian Walsh."

Chapter 17

Dora and Missy entered Mae's diner and were greeted by Pearlie Mae, who co-owned the diner with her wife, Winnie Chambers. Pearlie had fine, short, straight gray hair cut evenly, Dutch boy style, around her head. Her eyes were also gray and smiled in tandem with her mouth, which was highlighted by crimson lipstick.

"Ladies," she said in greeting.

"We're looking for—oh, never mind." Dora saw Sterling wave from a booth at the back of the diner and headed that way, nodding to the waitress, Caroline Trask, older sister of Catherine, the Beach City police lieutenant. Despite her look of perpetual exhaustion, Caroline claimed to enjoy serving customers, many of whom were regulars, at Mae's.

Sterling wore a white collared shirt, buttoned all the way to the top and black jeans.

"Can I buy you a coffee?" Dora asked as Caroline approached.

"Tea, please—green, if possible. No milk or sugar, thanks."

Caroline nodded that she'd heard.

Dora looked at Missy. "And Miss?"

"Coffee," Missy said.

"And two coffees," Dora added.

"Is it okay to ask," Missy began, as she rearranged her place setting, "about the circumstances around you meeting Lillian?"

Sterling smiled that same wry half smile Dora had noticed when they'd first met. "Well, you can ask," Sterling's eyes widened and looked back at Missy so directly that the latter looked down again at her place setting and began fiddling with her spoon.

"If that's too personal," Dora said, "we can take your suggestion and talk about Lillian."

"It's not too personal. I'm just not used to being asked."

"Sorry," said Missy.

"That's okay." Sterling stilled and smiled, this time more shyly. "I've been uncomfortable with the very idea of gender since as far back as I can remember. When I was like three, I remember being referred to as this cute little girl—and it made me mad."

Missy nodded; Dora waited.

"And I became this tomboy, but I didn't love it. I didn't seem to fit in anywhere on the gender spectrum. So when I learned, maybe six or seven years ago, that some people identify as nonbinary, I just knew that was me. And it was fine. The problem wasn't me—it was everyone else. I've had a hard time with other people—at jobs, family functions, nights out with friends—putting me in a gender box. So I got kind of used to being alone, and I'm fine with that." Sterling's blue eyes shone. "But it gets lonely, and I wanted some help navigating ways to be less lonely, and that's where W.A.R. came into the picture."

"Tell us about Lillian," Missy suggested.

Sterling nodded. "At first, Lillian and I were friends. I knew her from another part of my life, and she suggested that her organization could help me. I knew a little about her involvement there because we'd known each other awhile. When Lillian founded Women at Risk, it literally saved her life. She won the Third Annual County M.A.D.—Make a Difference—Award for her volunteer work with women. She did everything at first—managed the office and counseled the women who called or came in. Then Shelly showed up. She, too, was wonderful, and she and Lillian became best friends. I know this from both of them, since Shelly and I were close as well." Sterling's face had grown animated, excited, and Missy leaned forward, eager to hear more. Dora sat back, taking in Sterling's story more passively.

"Shelly, however, was not a woman by birth. She was a trans woman." Sterling looked from Dora to Missy. "And Lillian was religious, which wasn't a problem, at first. But Shelly knew a lot of trans women who felt unsafe and were abused and had traumatic backstories. So she started bringing them in, and the character of W.A.R. changed. The trans women—there were a few men, too, but mostly women—began to dominate the culture of the place, perhaps because their traumas were multileveled, or simply because Shelly knew so many of them. Woman at Risk was no longer the extension of her personality it had been. It was no longer…Lillian. And it was all because of Shelly."

Dora's eyes narrowed as Caroline arrived with the coffees and tea. "Will there be anything else?" She looked at each of them, all of whom shook their heads. "Enjoy," she said, and went on to another booth.

"Do you think Lillian wanted to control the—" Dora searched for the right word and settled on the one Sterling had used—"character of the place?"

"Maybe." Sterling nodded slowly. "Maybe not consciously, but I definitely think she felt threatened by Shelly—in part because Shelly's personality was so magnetic. She was the life of her salon and became the life of W.A.R."

"Were you a customer at Rainbow Salon?" Dora asked.

"Occasionally, yes."

"Did Lillian also dislike Lee?"

"She couldn't stand Lee." Sterling scoffed and looked from Dora to Missy, then back again. "And she positively hates me."

"Do you really think," Dora continued, "that Lillian's frustration at the changes at her organization might have led her to kill people?"

Sterling huffed a sardonic breath. "Have you met Lillian? The woman's a freight train—one-track mind and as intense as they come!"

"Well, that doesn't mean she killed anyone," Missy observed. Sterling didn't answer.

Once they had all finished their beverages, Sterling mentioned something about being needed back at work and left. Dora paid for the beverages, and she and Missy drove past the W.A.R. offices, where they saw Celia Worly directing William, who was loading a bulky duffle bag into the trunk of a car.

• • •

Ganderson found Mallard waiting for him in an interrogation room, arranging printouts of notes on the table. Ganderson was carrying a paper bag, which he set down on the table and from which he took two large cups of coffee, two enormous apple crumb muffins—Ganderson's favorite—and a small, somewhat stained stack of napkins.

"Keep them away from the evidence. We don't want to be getting crumbs all over everything." Mallard brushed off the papers nearest Ganderson's bag.

"There are no crumbs, and the printouts aren't evidence. We can always print the pages out again. Anyway, I just took the muffins out, so there aren't any crumbs." Ganderson broke the top off of one of the muffins and took a bite.

"Well, there are crumbs now, aren't there!" Mallard threw up his hands and turned his back to Ganderson.

"Okay!" Ganderson took the coffee, muffins, and napkins off of the table and placed them on one of the chairs that was bolted to the floor so as to keep it from becoming a weapon during interrogations.

"Look at the mess you made." Mallard pointed to the table, where there was a thin coffee ring and a sprinkle of crumbs.

Ganderson swiped the ring and crumbs with his hand toward the edge of the table. "Satisfied?"

Mallard shook his head, grumbling.

"Can we get to work please!" Ganderson begged.

Mallard held up both hands. "Okay. That's why I'm here, but we do need to keep our notes orderly. Disorderly notes means—"

"Disorderly investigation. I know. So what have we got?" Ganderson asked, shifting gears.

Mallard pointed at the images on the printout at the far left of the table.

"We've got matching boot prints. Military style, desert boots. List of suspects with images and details."

Ganderson looked at his partner hopefully. "Are the boots rare?"

Mallard shrugged. "Not particularly, but there's wear in them that's unique." He pointed to one of the printouts. "Here we have what appears to be the same boot print found near a tire print on the fringe of the parking lot behind the school where Women at Risk holds its meetings. If that's our truck, it would have been parked a bit off to the side. Perhaps to keep a distance from…a body?"

Mallard looked at Ganderson, but Ganderson's expression never changed. Mallard continued. "I'm thinking the killer had to squeeze the truck around the body, then climb up onto the fringe to get into the cab." He glanced again at Ganderson, then added, "Oh, and we have that sighting from across the street from the beach where Lee Travers was found of what looked to be a big guy carrying something over his shoulder early on the thirteenth."

Ganderson nodded but said nothing. He lifted his hand to the side of his head as if to smooth his hair back, but remembered that it was held in place with pomade and thought the better of it, and instead began scratching at a bit of acne on his cheek. "That's it, then?" he asked.

Mallard grinned and shot the cuffs of his six-hundred-dollar Brioni shirt. "Not quite." He took a piece of laser paper out of the inside of his jacket. "Look at what Benny Anderson and that kid—what's his name? Whippery—?"

"Whippley."

"Look what they found, hiding in the weeds at the Ocean Parkway site." He laid the paper on the table and smoothed it out. "Three seventy-five-grain hollow-point jackets from an AR-15."

Ganderson grinned, slapped the table, and stood up. He started to hug his partner but caught himself and slapped him on the back instead. "Holy crap!" he snorted.

"Right?" Mallard walked around to another side of the table. "We have bits of blue tarp fiber from the beach where the first body was found, from splinters under the boardwalk, and both kill locations." He picked up a piece of paper that was stapled to another behind it. "We also have both victim's phones. Shelly Borzer had calls from Barbara Skolnick, the Women at Risk office, and Winona Lofer's cell, among many others."

"Yeah," said Ganderson. "Everyone loved Shelly."

"Whereas Lee"—Mallard flipped to the second page and held the papers out to show Ganderson, who waved them away—"had calls from Shelly and Doug Szerbo."

Ganderson took one of the coffees and a muffin, along with several napkins, and sat down in one of the two remaining chairs. As he ate and sipped, he leaned back, deep in thought.

"And both their phones had a call from the same burner," Mallard said.

"I see that. Now shut up," Ganderson admonished. "I'm thinking."

Mallard leaned back against the wall, frowned, took off his Sebastian Lino tweed jacket and brushed the back of it, then put it back on.

Ganderson stood up, picked up one of the sheets, and slapped it with his other hand. "We need a closer look at Borzer's brother."

"He does have motive and opportunity in a major way, but the obvious question—" Mallard began.

Ganderson's gaze flicked to his partner. "What's Lorne Berger's tie to Lee Travers?"

Mallard took the remaining coffee and muffin, spread the bag out like a placemat on the remaining chair, sat down, and took a bite of the muffin. "Process of elimination." He held the muffin up. "Dry," he said, and took a long draw on his coffee, then made a face. "Bitter!"

Ganderson pouted derisively. "With the way you dress and the way you eat, you're in the wrong profession."

Mallard glanced back at him. "You sound like my wife. So Barbara Skolnick could handle an AR-15 and doesn't like people of indeterminate gender."

"Agreed, but not enough motive."

Ganderson peered at his partner. "Stick with Berger."

"Skolnick goes in the maybe column."

Ganderson moved a paper printed with Skolnick's name and photo off to one side.

"Same with Szerbo."

Ganderson did the same with Douglas Szerbo's page. "Do we know if that burner left messages?" he asked.

"Geekman's working on it. He says his software will recover deleted files on computers, phones and emails, as long as you get to the device fast—before it's written over. We'll find out soon."

Ganderson lifted his coffee, toasting his partner. "Here's hoping."

Chapter 18

After receiving anonymous input from the public following *The Chronicle's* RFI—Request for Information social media posts, Sarah Turner made two calls, the first to Detective Paul Ganderson, the second to Dora. Both calls relayed the same information—information that had been called in to her "news hotline" which, since she'd given birth to Olivia, forwarded to Sarah's cellphone. Several people had called in sightings of Ford F-150s—two of them dark blue, one black—whose owners had been behaving suspiciously, in the callers' opinions. None of the callers explained what that behavior was. The call about the black truck had been a sighting slightly west of the Women at Risk headquarters.

After making her calls, Sarah fed Livvie and laid her in her crib for a nap. Olivia seemed to know when Sarah was awake; that was the only time she seemed to sleep. She was awake, and often crying, late nights when Sarah and C3 were trying to sleep. C3 would be home soon; he spelled Sarah with Olivia in the afternoons, then returned to his job driving Uber in the evening.

• • •

After ending her call with Sarah, Dora decided to investigate the F-150 sighting nearest the W.A.R. headquarters. She drove to Beach City's business district and circled the neighborhood several times. She saw the truck as she turned the corner onto the headquarters' block following her third time around; her attention was drawn to it because a woman was leaning, face first, into the passenger's side window.

The woman was Lillian Walsh.

Dora pulled into a spot next to a fire hydrant not far from the truck and watched. The conversation went on for several minutes, at the end of which, Lillian nodded, turned, and went back into the building.

Dora pulled out of the spot and onto the road so she could see the truck's license plate. Then she drove back to Geller Investigations, pondering what she had just seen.

• • •

Mallard hung up the phone and explained to Ganderson why Sarah had called.

Ganderson rubbed the scars on his face and shook his head. "Do you have any idea how many Ford F-150s there are around here?"

Mallard conceded the point. He tapped his forefinger on the paper with the photo and identifying information for Lorne Berger. "I agree that he should be our focus. With his sister gone, that inheritance is his. And what's more, maybe his sister's money laundering connection's no coincidence. Maybe the inheritance, the laundering, and the murder are all part of the same narrative."

"How's the weather out on that limb you're on?" Ganderson smirked. "Maybe Lorne was just looking for his sister, like he said."

186

"Yeah well, maybe the money laundering hit a snag and Rivkin reached out from jail and had her killed."

Ganderson's expression implied he conceded the possibility.

Mallard's eyes were anxious and brooding. "I just keep getting hung up on the missing Lee Travers connection."

Ganderson barely paused. "Maybe she found out about or even witnessed the first murder."

Mallard brightened. "True. But there's the weapon. Not sure I'm buying that Lorne Berger would use an AR-15. Where could he get one, for one thing?"

Ganderson scoffed. His tone was scornful. "Where couldn't he get one?"

. . .

While Dora sat in front of her computer at her dining room table sorting through the information they had pertaining to the case, Missy was focused on her iPad, the tip of her tongue protruding slightly from the right corner of her mouth while she hummed Radiohead's song "Creep" softly to herself.

"Okay," she said, "the owner of the Ford F-150's name is Damian Wurtz. I plugged his plate into the DMV. He's also apparently well-known on gaming platforms by other names, except if you look closely, his information is on documents on screen, in the background. He lives just outside a place called Newcomb, near another town called Long Lake, way upstate."

"Good going, Miss."

Missy was looking back at her with a smile that was sanguine and sly. "I'm just getting started."

Dora didn't understand. "Well, what else can you—?"

"Dor." Missy shook her head and looked at her with an *Oh really?* expression. "I'm a librarian. Research."

"Can you do that over here," Dora asked, "so I can see?"

"I'm the one doing the work—you come here."

Dora gave a hearty laugh. "Touché!" She came over and sat down cross-legged on the floor next to Missy.

"When I'm done," Missy explained, "I'm going to be able to tell you all about this sucker."

"How?"

"Know what an IP address is?"

"Sure, in a general sense."

"We're looking in a specific sense. Given that this guy lives in a house, he probably has a static one. You know what cookies are?"

"Like Oreos? Just kidding—yes, also in a general sense."

"Well, as you probably know, websites keep track of visitors to try and sell them more stuff."

"It's all about the green," Dora commented.

"Exactly. And we can use that. See, ISPs—Internet service providers —own blocks of IP addresses, which are also recorded in public databases operated by regional Internet registries."

"Above my pay grade." Dora rubbed her forehead.

"Not mine." Missy grinned. "Anyway, there are only five registries, so getting hold of someone's ISP is as simple as plugging the IP address into the right database."

"But that's just the ISP," Dora observed. "What good is having only the service provider?"

"Good point. I'm glad you asked! I've found a program that will tell us which subscriber is associated with a particular IP address at the service provider—and best of all, the program will do that for both static and dynamic IP addresses. Just give me a few minutes."

Dora watched with admiration while Missy searched, downloaded, and analyzed. Finally, Missy sat back.

"Done?" Dora asked, not comprehending what she was seeing on Missy's iPad.

"Oh, no. We now have raw information—Wurtz's browsing history. We can learn a lot about him from that. For his physical history, of course, we'd have to drive upstate and tail him—probably with at least two cars. But browsing history—simple, for a librarian with some tech savvy and"—she blew on her nails—"maybe a degree in info science."

Dora squinted towards the iPad's screen, trying to read the names of the websites where Wurtz spent his time and which Missy was now visiting. Half an hour later, Missy looked at Dora, breathless. "Get all that?"

"Not remotely."

"This Wurtz is a bad, bad dude. He spends a lot of time visiting and participating in certain forums."

"What forums?"

"Well, they appear to all be splinter groups of a decentralized network. I need to dig a little more."

Dora shook her head. "And…?"

Missy said nothing as she read and clicked and read some more. When she looked at Dora, she was pale and frightened. "So you know that there are groups that congregate and grow on the Internet—people who hate Black people or Asians or Latinos or Jews or gay people or Arabs or non-binary—well, these people hate everything and everyone, and they're vitriolic and violent about it. Now mostly, they keep to themselves. They don't really want anything to do with anyone else. But their views are the extreme of the extremists, and they're all over the world. Not only that; they're militant and some of their members train in their own militias."

Now she had Dora's attention. "So what do they do—just train?"

"Well, yeah. They train. They believe that much of society is a threat to them. They believe that a lot of what's been accomplished—civil rights—is threatening to them. Sometimes they hire themselves out as mercenaries because they're willing to kill just about anyone. But it's got to be in line with their thinking. It's got to fit, so to speak, with their DNA."

Dora looked back at Missy for a long moment. "So what's this Wurtz guy doing so far away from his home territory?"

Missy shrugged. "The million-dollar question."

"And why would he be involved with a social worker who runs a network supporting women?"

• • •

"I don't know what you think we missed the first time," Mallard said as they entered what had been Shelly Borzer's home. The little cape was nestled between enormous lifted and dormered houses and was decorated very much the way one might expect of any single woman's home in the vicinity of a beach.

"Neither do I," Ganderson admitted. "I figure we'll know it when we see it. How 'bout you take the bedrooms and bath and I'll start in here and work my way to the kitchen?"

The living room featured paintings of sandy beaches and blue and green seas—of beach umbrellas and surf and boats and birds. Ganderson quickly rifled through the shelves on the wooden breakfront, which featured knickknacks, including lacquered driftwood, shells, small, elegant glass and metal sculptures. The matching coffee table was empty, save for books about 16th century art and sculpture and modern fashion— particularly up-to-date approaches to hair styling and coloring.

The kitchen drawer yielded nothing besides local restaurant menus, old pencils, paper clips and screwdrivers. A computer and iPad had been confiscated and examined during an earlier search.

Mallard had already searched the guest bedroom, which was clean and neat. The bed was covered with extra pillows and blankets. Shelving sported a variety of both fashion- and nature-related books. Several minutes after he began searching Shelly's bedroom, he called out: "Got something."

Ganderson started toward the bedroom and nearly ran into Mallard, who was coming toward him in the hallway. The latter was holding two pieces of light beige stationery in his gloved hand. The detectives stood just inside the living room's bay window, examining the pages.

"'Dear Steven,'" Mallard read aloud. "'I thought it made sense to try and explain my efforts to have Paula removed from the will. Nearly all of the money that was left to us was either inherited or earned by Dad. Camille and Paula weren't even on the scene, so in my view while yes, Camille as his second wife is deserving of a half share, Paula is not. She was never part of the family. She ignored every Thanksgiving, Christmas, and Easter dinner invitation and never called, much less visited, for either of our birthdays. The tough times you had, during which we all supported you—yes, even Camille—with your struggles might as well never have occurred as far as Paula was concerned. The fact that she was in Camille's will was Camille's doing, of course, but the fact of the matter is, she deserves nothing, given that just about all of this was Dad's money. I know you've said the money's not important, and you've always been willing to give everyone everything they want, but sometimes that's not fair to others. In this case, giving Paula even a half share of the money is wrong. It hurts me, and it hurts you. I'm willing to concede regarding Camille, because Dad loved her and she was there for us, but not Paula. She'd have nothing to do with Dad, nor with us. Do what you have to do, but I will do everything I can to see to it that Paula gets nothing, because nothing is what she deserves. I hope you are well. Love, Your brother Lorne.'"

"So…a step-sister," Ganderson declared, wiping a palm over his nose and mouth.

"Paula." Mallard nodded. "And Lorne doesn't sound like he was out to get Shelly." He sat down on the couch, and Ganderson sat next to him, his face still, thoughts churning. "When was it postmarked?"

"A few days after he came to us," Ganderson said. "I guess right after their stepmother died. I still think you're too trusting. Maybe all this is what he wants us to think."

Mallard raised an eyebrow, then held up a hand. "You think that when he came to us, the whole story about looking for his brother was a smokescreen?"

Ganderson shrugged. "Could be."

Mallard continued. "He sends this letter, then goes and kills Shelly and keeps the money. So where's Paula?"

"Maybe he killed Paula too. I mean, there's an inheritance. There's loads of motive. Where is she? I'll tell you what we need to do is get in touch with the lawyers handling the estate. Then we'd see who's been laying claim. We'd know pretty quick if this Paula's around." Ganderson snorted; his mouth was a tight line, his lips invisible. "Were there any other letters back there?"

"No, there was just—wait, the mailbox!" Mallard hurried to the front door, opened it, and rushed outside. He came back with a bulging, diverse pile of envelopes in one hand, while waving a single, sealed, number ten envelope over his head in the other. He lay the pile of envelopes off to one side of the coffee table, the newly found envelope in the middle. *P. Ricci* was printed in dark red on the top left of the front of the envelope above the address of an apartment in Beach City. The envelope was addressed to Shelly Borzer.

"The guys didn't check the mailbox. I don't think we can open mail belonging to a dead person," Mallard said.

Ganderson huffed a laugh. "Doesn't matter."

"Why's that?" Mallard wanted to know.

Ganderson slid a gloved finger beneath the flap on the back and opened the envelope. "Because it's already open." He removed the letter and sat back, holding it so that they both could read it. "This isn't HIPAA," he muttered, as they both began to read, "pretty sure privacy rights only apply to the living."

"So Paula knew about Steven's change to Shelly," Mallard said, "but apparently the brother Lorne didn't."

Ganderson agreed. "Tells us Paula probably got along with Shelly, or at least wasn't completely rejected as she was by Lorne."

"And she doesn't seem to care about the money," Mallard pointed out.

"But her mother cared," said Ganderson. "Makes sense. That's how mothers are—always thinking of their kids' futures."

Mallard's phone burred. He answered, listened, hung up, then turned to Ganderson. "Got a match on that dried hock of phlegm at the Borzer scene by Ocean Parkway."

"Yeah?"

"Belongs to a sicko named Damian Wurtz, who also has a bunch of aliases, upstate, not too far from the Canadian border."

Ganderson looked intrigued. "Wonder what he's doing way down here."

Chapter 19

You live much of your life on the wrong side of the law—and you're proud of that. You move often. For the most part, the law is an invasion of the personal freedoms guaranteed you by the United States Constitution, that document that has been, perhaps more misunderstood than any other, with the possible exception of the Bible.

To the degree you interact with anyone, you're part of a loose community of more or less like-minded people, all of whom live outside of the boundaries of the law, all of whom agree upon their God-given rights to absolute freedom, and most of whom agree upon their duty to take whatever action they deem necessary when their rights are infringed upon.

You and others refer to your community as The People, as in We the People—and The People share information about resources, one of which is available living spaces—usually apartments that are located in homes owned by one or more of The People. Rentals of these living spaces are one of the ways by which The People earn their living. Rentals are on a month-to-month or week-to-week—somedays even day-to-day —basis. Whatever is agreed upon by those involved.

You stay ahead of whatever government agency, department or representative might be after you for any one of a number of infringements—though you do not consider your actions infringements. They're exercises of your rights. You can live the way you see fit, and to hell with anyone who tries to stand in your way. You just make sure to be forever off the grid.

Currently you live in a studio apartment in a home owned by Don and Connie—you don't know their last names and don't want to know. Don is part owner of a junk yard, which figures prominently in your life —not as part of your employment, but in another way.

You're a self-employed welding contractor—oxyacetylene and arc welding. You'd purchased your own equipment decades earlier and continue to put it to good use. You have a variety of customers—some are automotive-related, though most are used farm equipment dealers who are solo entrepreneurs like yourself. You also do a little business with a few industrial concerns—people you don't like very much because they're part of conglomerates built on structures comprised of rules. You hate rules. But you can take advantage of their rules by billing according to them. They pay well.

Your apartment smells of old socks and body odor and your dog, but none of that bothers you except when you come in from outdoors; you don't like showering or washing your clothes. Why should you? Both are wastes of time that most people engage in far too much. They also waste water—a vital natural resource that's fast evaporating because people are, in your opinion, washing themselves and their clothing far too much. The problem contributes to the burning, if it is really occurring and is not fake news—of the western United States, the best part of the United States.

You have no opinion on climate change. Whatever the temperature is outside, you know how to take care of yourself.

Your apartment's a mess except for an area along one south-facing wall that's eight feet wide and begins at desk level and rises to just below the ceiling. The area is beautifully decorated with red and purple wall tapestries, several scrolls, two fake diplomas and equally fake awards—all of which, despite being fake, contain very real information so you can reference them, and people would know these awards had been bestowed upon a very real Damian Wurtz. Directly facing this decorated area is a computer on which is mounted a very good web cam; another equally good web cam is mounted slightly off to one side.

You're not only known as Damian Wurtz—you're also known as DWDefcon and DTactikel in the gaming universe—your preferable universe. You're an extremely high-level gamer. You'd begun playing the original Titanfall game about five years earlier, using the Xbox your mom had bought you years earlier. You'd not have used the word "playing" to describe your use of the game, nor would you have used the word "game." You *live* the games, you don't *play* them. The universe, the "real" universe is the one you "play." The "games" *are* real life. "Real life" is the game.

Titanfall is a first-person shooter game, and it was where your love of guns blossomed into a hunger for automatic weapons, eventually the AR-15 you thought of as "your sweet baby." That's not to say that Titanfall caused your hunger; it was simply where your desire took hold.

You were a natural at Titanfall and your success evolved into renown and, ultimately, legend. You began playing on the Twitch platform, where people pay to watch you play, and where you make a growing percentage of your living.

Eventually you began playing a related game called Apex Legends, a hero-royale game where players are grouped into squads that do battle. You are DTactikel there, and so skilled and successful that other gamers clamor to join your squads. Here again, you earn money through play-ing-as-performance.

When you game, you sit in front of the little designed and decorated section of your apartment—your own virtual universe that's further dec-orated within each game.

When you're not gaming, you spend some of your time in junkyards, including the one owned by your current landlord and his wife. Because you're a welder, your presence in junkyards would appear to most to be reasonable. What might seem less reasonable is what you spend most of your time doing in the junkyards—practicing shooting your AR-15. You work on your shooting the way you worked on your virtual shooting and other gaming skills—with a drive born of obsession. The automatic weapon was drowned out in the junkyards by the din of the yard, and what wasn't drowned out was absorbed or blocked by the mountains of metal and rubber. You practice at Don's yard and also at another yard owned by the Andralone brothers, whose two Great Danes, Crag and Farg, roam the yard. The brothers had concerns that you might acciden-tally shoot the dogs if they rounded a corner of a mountain of junk too quickly. Kill dogs? What kind of person did they think you were? You understood and were careful, though you didn't have to worry so much at Don's yard, since Don didn't have dogs, so you spent most of your time there. It was all about Freedom.

Your third means of income was doing what were referred to as "Tasks" for individuals you met through The People network, some of whom, for reasons that were none of your business, decided to exercise their rights by ridding the world of one or more of its inhabitants—usually extremists of one kind or another.

You believe that much of society's a menace to the freedoms and rights you and others of your ilk share. You agree that government at all levels is inherently dangerous, as is anyone who advocates for the infringement of any rights, belongings, freedoms, weapons, actions or income—anyone who claims that their rights depend on any reduction of yours.

The first Task was a challenge—you had to push yourself; the second time was easier, but you found yourself resisting an extremely addictive exhilaration.

But only slightly.

Chapter 20

Charlie and Dean Clayburgh were drinking in Charlie's office with the doors closed. It was well into the second shift, and proofs from earlier in the day and evening were scattered around Charlie's desk. They'd looked at them and forwarded their comments to the outer, production room where Vanessa was working with Luis on the latest versions of the ads. Charlie was pretty sure he'd heard another voice coming from the outer room, which doubled as the Bernelli Group's studio.

The voice belonged to Lorne Berger, who was the face of their HelthE Snax product and ad campaign, and who apparently had something going with Vanessa, his office manager.

Charlie looked at his Apple Series 6 Watch, and said, "It's ten now. How 'bout we go to eleven, eleven thirty?"

Clayburgh smiled a pissing contest of a smile. He made a show of looking at his watch, a brand-new Apple Series 7, and said, "How 'bout we play it by ear?"

Charlie, who understood the nature of their relationship, said, "You got it, pal," and went back to work on his scotch. He'd made sure to leave a little bit in the bottle—which was their second of the evening, and the last of the single malt. He knew his place; the last of the bottle always goes to the client.

He caught Clayburgh's eye and nodded toward the bottle. Clayburgh nodded back and poured the rest into his glass. Charlie had a little ice in his glass and Clayburgh snorted at the notion that anyone needed his single malt over ice. Everything was about dominance on some level, and he was a pro at pissing contests. He always had the biggest dick.

Charlie's phone rang. He looked at it, said, "The wife" to Clayburgh, and let it ring. Eventually, it stopped, then rang again.

"Better get it," Clayburgh said.

"You're right," Charlie agreed. "Hey," he said into the phone. He listened.

Clayburgh muttered, "Pussy whipped."

"So I'm looking at an article in *The Chronicle*," Christine was saying, "and there are no new facts about the murders or the victims, which I understand, but these articles are really just about the other articles."

Charlie sipped his scotch and made a mock-woeful expression for Clayburgh's benefit. "Well," he drawled, "they've gotta sell advertising, don't forget. The ads will pay for two weeks in Turks and Caicos in January."

"The point is," Christine went on—she was building up steam, "it isn't helpful for anyone—yes, perhaps excepting her advertisers—for Sarah to print articles that say, 'Hey, remember yesterday's article about murder victim number two's life that wasn't very relevant? Here's what you *really* need to know about her—which also isn't very relevant.' There's no reason for her to print such a story except PR, and come on, that's outweighed by the damage to summer traffic, to beach attendance, to tourism, to local businesses, restaurants, bars, and what have you. Printing a story like that in her paper is in no one's interest!"

Charlie rolled his eyes, making sure Clayburgh could see. "Sarah doesn't print *anything*. It's all on the Internet." He giggled.

"How much have you had to drink?" Christine demanded. "Are you with that client?"

Charlie knew that his wife didn't like Clayburgh, who she thought was vacuous, while she was anything but. His wife, the mayor of Beach City, was as principled a person as he'd ever known. She was a regular churchgoer who adored and utterly surrendered to Jesus, and maintained principles that she believed were in line with her religion, which, she maintained, was the most important relationship in her life, and which determined the nature of all of her other relationships. Christine's principles were quite possibly the reason Charlie had married her, but there could be too much of a good thing! They had been high school sweethearts eventually driven apart by his alcoholism—though he was quick to point out that she enjoyed her wine. They had multi-layered ties that bound them—ties that were many decades old.

"If it's any comfort, babe, I feel the same. Sarah takes her journalism too far. I suppose you want me to try to get C3 to influence her to tone it down?"

Christine sighed. "If I wanted C3's help, I'd ask him myself. He wouldn't react well to you trying to get him to do anything with Sarah."

He had expected she would back off if he suggested stepping in. "I was gonna say that."

"I'm just blowing off steam," she said.

"I know it. You need to have faith that it's going to be okay—the beach season, the tourism. Look, it's all picking up, now that COVID is less of a problem."

"Yup," she said, somewhat buoyed by the points he'd made. They ended the call.

Charlie was in fact thinking about calling C3 to try to convince him to talk to Sarah. He had also not checked in on his granddaughter in a few hours. He was obsessed with Olivia and the fact that she was a child with special needs. He felt a deeply biological compulsion to protect her.

"Got another?" Clayburgh was holding up the empty scotch bottle.

"Gonna have to slum it," Charlie answered—his way of saying they would have to give up drinking the single malts, now that his top shelf stash was gone. He opened the office door and went out into the production room, where Luis was working and Vanessa was essentially pinned against a wall by Lorne Berger, who was pressing himself against her. Charlie ignored them and went to a cabinet, where he hunted around for a moment and took out the best bottle of Irish whiskey he could find.

Clayburgh had followed Charlie out of the office, drink in hand, packets of his HelthE Snax in the other. He laid the Snax on each of the desks, then looked over Luis's shoulders.

"Love it!" he crowed, and Luis grinned over his shoulder at the client.

"Sorry to hear about your brother," he said, loudly enough so that Lorne could hear.

"Sister," Lorne said, looking annoyed to be distracted from Vanessa.

"Oh," Clayburgh sounded confused, "I thought—"

"Sister!" Lorne angrily insisted, and Charlie's head whipped around toward the man who was apparently verbally assaulting his client.

"Vanessa—" Charlie warned, implying that she should deal with Lorne.

Vanessa slid out from between Lorne and the wall and walked toward the exit. "Let's go get a drink," she said to Lorne and walked out the exit to the stairs.

"Hey," Lorne called, and he followed, which had been her intention all along.

• • •

Whatever was going on between them continued at Rudy's, where they found a spot at the crowded bar.

"You can't be like that around clients," Vanessa tried to explain. "They pay Charlie, who pays you and pays me." Something was obviously going on with him. *Could it be he was bothered that she had rebuffed his advances at her job? In front of other people?* She'd known guys who got crazy when they were rebuffed even a little bit.

"Let me tell you something," Lorne said with a withering stare that was, to Vanessa, a little unhinged. "People have to shut up about Shelly. They think they know about her because she changed, but they don't know shit. If they didn't know her, they need to shut the fuck up. That"—he gestured toward Rudy's front door, but he meant Dean Clayburgh—"that jackass had nothing to do with Shelly, so he should keep his mouth shut!" He was shouting now and didn't see the customers surrounding the couple who were starting to turn and stare; he also didn't see Rudy glaring in his direction.

Vanessa tried to diffuse Lorne's volatility. "But Lorne, nobody's trying to—"

"And you know what? So should you. So! Should! You!" He was jabbing a finger into her collarbone when suddenly he found his finger grasped by Rudy's massive fist.

"Not in my place," Rudy growled.

Lorne glared back.

"And not her. You mess with her"—Rudy nodded toward Vanessa—"you're messing with me." He thrust his head close to Lorne's. "Bad idea," he muttered.

Lorne's eyes were wide. "Yeah? Yeah?" was all he said, as Rudy thrust Lorne's finger and hand away from him.

"We're done," Vanessa said evenly to Lorne, who looked from Vanessa to Rudy and back again. Then he turned and left the bar.

• • •

Mallard pressed the doorbell beside the front door of the house listed as P. Ricci on the envelope they'd found at Shelly Borzer's apartment. After a few moments, he pressed it again. They waited.

"Try it again," Ganderson advised. He did.

"One more time," Ganderson insisted after they'd waited a minute or two.

Mallard complied, then looked at Ganderson, eyebrows raised.

"Let's get back to the station and discuss, then maybe see the brother," Ganderson said.

They returned to the station and again went over everything they had, at Ganderson's insistence. That, and three iced coffees later, Paul Ganderson was pacing back and forth, with all their information laid out on the table.

"Would you stop that?" Mallard begged. "You're making me dizzy. Let's sit down at the desks and chill."

They sat with their eyes closed for a few moments.

"Okay, one more time," Mallard offered. "What do we have?" He was trying to placate Ganderson, whose obsession with the details of the case was skyrocketing. Mallard suspected his partner's blood pressure was skyrocketing as well.

Ganderson refocused on the facts. "We have two siblings who were to share in an inheritance."

"Two and a half," Mallard corrected. "And the half was probably shut out and seems to be missing, while one of the other two's been brutally murdered."

Ganderson continued. "We also have another victim who was acquainted with the first but is not necessarily part of the inheritance picture, and whose killing is sketchy, motive-wise."

"The only thing I can think of is that Lee Travers somehow found out about what really happened to Shelly Borzer. They did know one another."

"Yeah, they did. And we have DNA from this peckerhead from upstate who has nothing to do with anything except he's crazy, and not in a benign way."

Mallard considered this. "Hired gun?"

"Who the hell knows? What do we know really about this guy? Not much."

Mallard brightened. "Here's a crazy idea—what if Lee really *was* Paula Berger Ricci?"

"You know what?" Ganderson said.

"You like that?"

"No!" Ganderson was emphatic. "Like you said—it's crazy."

The detectives looked at one another, then Ganderson snapped his fingers, picked up the phone, and dialed a two-digit intercom number while reaching for the envelope that had held the letter from P. Ricci. "I have a letter from a P. Ricci," he said into the phone. "Could she be one of the unlisted incoming or outgoing calls from Shelly Berger's phone?" He listened for a moment, then said, "Let me know."

"Geekman?" Mallard asked.

Ganderson nodded. "Shelly Borzer talked to the immediate world."

Mallard asked, "How can it be that Paula, Lorne, and Shelly all lived right here, and yet they communicated only by mail?"

Ganderson said, "Do you get along with all your relatives? Are there some you don't see and maybe don't want to see, so maybe you'd send a letter, especially if what you need to talk about isn't so pleasant? And maybe you might want to leave a paper trail."

"A paper trail," Mallard mused. "But this wasn't sent registered."

"And another thing. They live in separate parts of Beach City. The middle part of town, where Lorne lives, is off the beach, whereas the west end, where Shelly lived, is like the Jersey Shore—all bars and restaurants and night life, whereas Paula lived in the walks, which is its own little community. And anyway, she obviously wants to stay clear of Lorne. Sounds like she's afraid of Lorne."

The phone rang. Mallard picked it up. He listened for a minute, took a pen from his shirt pocket, scribbled something on the envelope in front of him, then hung up. "Paula Ricci's number. Geekman got it from Shelly Berger's phone. I say we call her."

"Hang on," Ganderson said, holding up a palm. "Let's not scare her further."

"We need to talk to Lorne Berger," Mallard suggested.

"Agreed."

Ganderson retrieved Berger's address from Lieutenant "Re" Morse, and they went out into the parking lot. Outside, the sky was dark and threatening, and the wind had picked up.

"Whoa." Ganderson put his hands to the sides of his head to keep the wind from mussing his hair, which was unlikely given the amount of pomade he used to keep it in place. He hated when his hair, or anything else of his, was out of place.

They arrived at the two-story home on the residential street one block south of the main drag. The house was painted blue-gray with white trim. A small boat trailer sat at the back of the driveway behind a five-year-old red Dodge Durango and a new forest green Hyundai Sonata.

They walked up the four steps to the front door and rang the top of the two bells, then waited.

"He rents the second floor?" Ganderson wanted to know.

Mallard nodded.

The door opened, the officers introduced themselves and, after a brief discussion, Lorne Berger led them up the flight of stairs that was just inside and to the right of the doorway to the home's second floor. The home's owner had, like many others in the neighborhood, adapted the second floor into a standalone apartment, which was rented to people wanting to live walking distance from the beach. Such rentals could bring many thousands of dollars per month in rent, particularly during the spring and summer months.

"Coffee?" Berger asked.

The detectives declined. They sat around the table in the dinette, which was an extension of the kitchen.

"You have new information for me?" he wanted to know.

Mallard laid the letters on the table in front of Berger, who picked them up and read them. "So?" he said when he was finished.

"So you and your sisters are supposed to split an inheritance," Mallard said, "and now one of them's dead, leaving you with a bigger share."

"Where's Paula?" Ganderson asked, leaning toward Berger, who glared back at the detective.

"I'd like to know that myself, but I don't."

"If something happened to her," Ganderson continued, "you're left with all the money."

"And some explaining to do," Mallard added.

Berger pressed his palms to the top of the table. "I guess the first part's true, but first of all, I don't know where Paula is and have no reason to think she's not perfectly fine, probably at home."

"We've been there," Ganderson began, but Berger interrupted him.

"And second of all, my sister Shelly's death was a tragedy."

"Your sister's death," Mallard countered, "was a murder."

"How 'bout you do your job and find out who did it?" Berger retorted.

"That's why we're here," Ganderson said quietly.

Berger looked at the two detectives, his face reddening with rage. "You bastards got anything else? Remember—I came to you."

"That would be a pretty decent smokescreen," Mallard observed.

Berger stood up. "If you're not going to arrest me, you need to leave."

Chapter 21

Dora left a key under the heart-shaped rock at end of the parking lot farthest from the rear of her apartment building. The key was for Janey, the dog walker she and Missy had begun sharing. The dogs, Dora's Freedom and Missy's Comfort, were together in her apartment; the walker would take them out, then feed them and take them out once more later on, while she was first at Geller Investigations, then at Vanessa's, sitting for her two boys. Missy was working at the library and would meet her later.

The dogs had their respective favorite toys: Freedom had a little rainbow striped ball which she nudged around the apartment, bounding after it whenever it rolled. Comfort had a paper plate. He had no understanding of balls or fetching, but he could spent hours tearing paper plates and paper towels, especially those bearing crumbs and remnants of food, into shreds. Comfort adored paper products.

Dora had come to the conclusion that her life with Missy had become so complicated and intertwined that moving in together was probably inevitable. She told herself that the move would be for convenience's sake rather than love. Though it had been several years since Franny's murder, it was too soon for her to dwell on loving anyone, even Missy, for very long. She could express love, be affectionate, even make love with Missy. But talking about it was different. Somehow, talking about love with Missy made their relationship too tangible and overwhelming.

She sighed. She knew she was not an easy person to love.

She arrived at the Geller Investigations office and was pleased to find Adam there. She knew he'd been sick, though she knew almost nothing about prostate cancer, nor what he was going through. Thelma was no help; the office manager barely acknowledged Dora when she walked in, and was invariably resistant to any of her suggestions on any subject.

Adam was at his desk, pecking away at his computer keyboard with two fingers.

"Divorce case?" Dora asked as she took the notebook marked "Sawyer Townsend" from a shelf and opened it to the last page. She began scanning the information in the book, working backwards from the end, reminding herself of the facts of the case from their investigation's point of view.

"Deadbeat dad," he answered, without looking up. "Guy moves faster than I can track him."

"Need help?"

"Nope."

Dora thought she heard Thelma's derisive laugh and the words "need help" mockingly repeated, and barely fought an impulse to respond aggressively.

Adam looked terribly haggard—exhausted—but before Dora could comment further, the front door banged open.

"Ellison here?"

She recognized Paul Ganderson's voice. He strode through the door to the back room, where she and Adam were working.

"Why don't you come in, Detective?" Thelma asked sarcastically.

"Don't mind if we do," said Mallard, who trailed his partner.

Ganderson wore the same brown suit he always wore; his hair glistened with pomade, and the acne on his face looked freshly picked. Mallard, on the other hand, was impeccably overdressed in some European fashionista's idea of an A-list's attire for a night out.

Ganderson strode over to where Dora was sitting, crowding her space and standing inches from her. He looked down at her; her face was at his belt level.

"You need to keep away from anyone relating to the Borzer and Travers murders." He pointed angrily into her space.

Dora eyed his finger. "You need to step away, Officer, or you'll lose more than that finger."

Ganderson's voice was low and threatening. He bent low, his face ugly with anger, thrust close to hers. "Threatening a police officer? Don't ever, ever tell me what to do! You've impeded our case from day one, when you asked Lorne Berger about his sister and opened his eyes to our investigation."

Dora was calm; she relished conflict. "I'm doing my job. You need to do yours without expecting the world to revolve around you."

"Okay, folks," Mallard exclaimed. "Er, ah—let's everyone take it down a notch, before we're all in too deep to, ah, de-escalate."

Ganderson stood up and brushed off the front of his jacket. "Stay away from Lillian Walsh and her organization—which includes Celia Worly and their clientele. And stay away from Lorne Berger."

Adam rose from his seat. He looked at Mallard, then shot Ganderson a look that was more doleful than angry. Ganderson was still red-faced, eyes bulging, a mini roadmap of veins standing out on his forehead, nose, and neck.

"Come on, Paul. I've got Dora working well within the confines of the law and decorum. I have every confidence that you and Gerry can get your case solved and Dora can get to the bottom of our client's needs without any of you banging into one another."

Ganderson was still standing over Dora, who stood up, yet remained inches from the detective.

"You're in a private office, Detective," she said evenly, "and you're harassing its employees."

"Come on, Paul," Mallard said, stepping to the doorway. "You've made your point. We have someplace to be."

Still breathing hard, Ganderson looked down so that he was nearly nose to nose with Dora. "You watch it, lady. I'm watching you."

Dora smiled. "Keep watching, Officer. I'll wave now and then."

"It's detective," Ganderson muttered, then turned and stalked past his partner.

"Well, wasn't that nice?" Thelma intoned after a long silence. She was watching from her usual perch in the doorway.

Adam looked at Dora with something resembling affection.

Dora wished she could think of something comforting to say, but she knew he wouldn't want her calling attention to his cancer.

"What's next on the case?" he asked.

"Going to see Lillian Walsh at Women at Risk."

"Oh, the cops'll love that," Thelma wryly observed.

Adam laughed loud and long—the best medicine, Dora thought.

• • •

As she drove to Women at Risk, where she was to meet Missy in the parking lot, Dora wondered if the detectives knew about Damian Wurtz, and if so, what they might know. While at the office, she had done a database search for him and found DMV and several warrants that pointed to an upstate address, but she had also found information suggesting that the address was owned by and rented to individuals other than Mr. Wurtz.

She had called the Women at Risk office and asked for Lillian and was told that Ms. Walsh was "in a meeting," which was fine with Dora, since she'd only wanted to confirm that Lillian was at the office. Of course, it was possible that the answer was a subterfuge, and Lillian was not, in fact, at the office. She would take that chance.

She found Missy waiting outside.

"Everything okay with the walker?" Missy asked.

"I guess. I left the key. The dogs were fine—goofing around when I left."

Once they'd arrived and parked in the business district, they knocked on the office door, which was answered by Celia Worly, who bent close to the door, which she'd opened a crack.

"Can we speak with Lillian, please?"

"Ms. Walsh is in a meeting," Worly said stiffly.

"I'm looking at her," Dora said, nodding toward the inner office through the half-open blinds on the door. "She's on the phone."

"It's a phone meeting," Worly protested.

"We have information," Missy explained, "pertaining to Shelly Borzer's murder—information Lillian will want to know about."

"Well—" Worly hesitated, then held the door open.

Despite her office manager's protests, Lillian held up a wait-a-minute finger to the two investigators and ended her call after several minutes. "Come in. Sit down," she said, sliding a second chair to the spot beside her desk.

Dora, who had been carrying the casebook from the office, took an ink-jetted photo from an inside pocket. "Do you recognize this man?"

Lillian examined the picture, then shook her head.

"He drives a black Ford-150," Dora prodded.

Lillian shrugged. "There was a guy in a black truck—I think he had red hair, might've had a beard. I don't remember. Was hanging around outside—more than once, which was disturbing, so I went out to ask what he wanted, told him I'd call the cops if he was around and that he had no business here." She looked from Dora to Missy. "Can't have anyone scaring our women…"

"How'd he seem?"

Lillian shrugged. "I don't really remember. It was a while ago."

"Did he threaten you?"

She shook her head. "Didn't seem that interested, frankly. Why?"

"Did you call the police?" Dora asked.

Lillian again shook her head. "No reason to—just a guy who was around. First two times I saw him were outside the school, and it was just before or after a meeting, so I thought he was picking up or dropping off one of the women. He was a positive. Then I saw him here, and that was weird. Anyway, calling the cops has never gotten me anywhere before. Stalwell's okay but in way over his head down there. I've dealt with Waycrest, the number two guy, but he's an entitled asshole who serves only those with the influence to make him look good, not a bunch of so-called 'scared women.'"

Once they were outside, Dora said, "Let's sit in the car." Once in the car, she asked, "Do you believe her?"

Missy said, "She's either telling the truth or she's really smart and is a really good actress."

"Maybe Celia Worly's involved. Maybe that's why the truck was around."

"Could be, I guess. Or maybe," Missy said, looking pointedly at Dora, "we need to find out more about Damian Wurtz."

• • •

"How was work tonight?" Dora asked later that evening when Vanessa returned.

"Exhausting," Vanessa answered. "Boys okay?"

"They're great. They explained to me all about their favorite shows, Motown Minis and Dinobots."

"We're doing a special ad campaign for Sawyer Townsend and the Rainbow Salon—a tribute to Shelly Borzer. We're calling it Shelly—Everybody's Friend."

"Nice." Dora smiled.

"And Charlie spent pretty much the whole night in his office, obsessively googling 'parenting children with special needs.'"

"That's Charlie," Dora observed, still smiling.

Then Vanessa explained to Dora about Lorne's attack; she'd avoided the subject when Dora had first arrived because she had to leave for work and didn't know how long the conversation would take.

"Give me his number," Dora said.

"No."

"Give me his address."

"No. I can handle this."

"How?"

Vanessa explained that she'd blocked Lorne on her phone and was having Charlie or Luis walk her to her car. When she arrived at work, she didn't leave her car until she saw that the coast was clear, and she'd been varying the times she came in.

"Charlie good with that?"

"It was Charlie's idea. He told Lorne that if he messes with me, he'll take him off the campaign and use stock images and videos. He would have booted Lorne anyway, except we're pretty deep into the campaign. Snax boxes have already been printed. Anyway, that seems to have backed him off. He's really vain and loves being part of the campaign. Loves modeling in general."

"And that all's working, you say?"

"So far. Now and then my phone seems to forget he's blocked, and I see that he's calling, but I just ignore it."

Chapter 22

When you'd first been given the Task, you thought immediately of a bomb. Bombs were so easy. Gaining access to just about anywhere, given a little ingenuity, was no trouble at all. People with responsibility were often lazy. You just had to watch them and spot test any security surrounding the target. Test a little here. Push a little there. Then watch the response. You'd know, assuming you had a brain and the knack. And you certainly had the knack.

These were some bizarre people, and you knew early on you were doing the world a service by getting rid of them.

You followed the targets, learned the routines, then took them out. Easy as pie. You just had to be patient. You had to wait, make sure no one was around.

You decided to use the AR-15—to send a message by targeting their privates. Let the world know you don't mess with what God gave you. While this wasn't part of the Task, you had the authority to make your own choices, as long as the Task got done.

So you bided your time. You were one of dozens of people you know with similar weapons and abilities who did similar Tasks for hire. It was not a big deal—and in this case, a public service. Get paid, identify your target and weapon, locate your target, wait for opportunity, get your ducks in a row. Take 'em down. Get the fuck out of there. Don't make a big production of it. Not all that hard if you knew what you were doing.

And you liked killing these people. They didn't belong. Eliminating them was God's work. Or maybe Darwin. Natural selection. You like that. What was this world coming to? We have men who want to be women, women who want to be men, people who say they're neither. Something had to be done, and here you've stumbled onto a Task that was actually a doorway into doing something about it. And best of all, you're being paid to do it. If that wasn't God's will…

You check your messages and notice an alert that has just come in. People are making inquiries—people who could cause you and others problems. Steps will have to be taken.

• • •

"I have a suggestion," Missy said. She was sipping tea while looking at her phone, where she had been working on an "expert level" Sudoku for a little over an hour. Dora was looking through their case notes. She looked up.

"I'd like to get a better sense of Celia Worly."

"A better sense of Celia Worly," Dora repeated. As if in response, Freedom, who had been lying next to Dora on the floor, raised her head. Dora stroked behind her ear. "That makes sense." Dora grinned.

"I'll call her now and see if she can meet us," Missy suggested.

"Sounds like a plan," Dora agreed blithely.

• • •

Celia Worly had agreed to meet Dora and Missy at Mae's Diner. They sat in one of the plush red and turquoise vinyl-covered booths. Dora, who wore workout shorts and tended toward overheating, liked the feel of the cool vinyl on the backs of her legs. Missy wore a mocha-colored cotton lawn cloth dress with white polka dots and a v-neck that Dora found surprisingly daring. Worly's hair was long and dark and cinched together at the back of her neck. She had sand-colored skin and wore a yellow cotton sleeveless dress with white bands at the shoulders and neck. Dora couldn't help noticing the movements of people in the diner reflected as blurs of light in the metallic ceiling.

They were waited on by Winnie Chambers, who was a part owner of the diner, which had been at auction after the previous owner, Horace Cobb, had been arrested as part of the corruption and murder scandal that had rocked the town several years earlier. Winnie was slow-moving, polite, gregarious and easy-going, a welcome combination as long as one was not too hungry and anxious for one's food to arrive.

"Well, how are you ladies today?" Winnie's honey-colored wrinkles coalesced into a smile that seemed to warm the booth as much as the spring sun coming through the wide window.

"How's your new dog gettin' along with Missy's?"

"Her last owner was an easy act to follow," Dora mused.

"So I heard," Winnie said.

"How's Pearlie?" Missy asked.

"Pearlie's Pearlie. Doin' her thing in the kitchen." Winnie laughed. "You know how marriage can be." She squinted from Dora to Missy and back again. "Well maybe you don't … yet." She glanced at Celia Worly, as though waiting to be introduced.

"Could we get…" Dora paused and mouthed "coffee?" to Celia, who nodded, "three coffees please, unless Miss—you want tea?"

"Coffee today, thanks," Missy said. "We're working hard."

Winnie's intimacy vanished, and she returned to her professional remove. "Three coffees coming up." She waddled away.

"So," said Worly, once Winnie was gone, "you want to know about Lillian? I'll tell you about Lillian. She founded W.A.R.—Women at Risk—six years ago, and it gave her purpose. I believe that the place literally saved her life. She won the County's Third Annual M.A.D. Award for her volunteer work with women."

"So we've heard," Dora interjected.

"Well, her organization helped a lot of women and probably saved more than a few. She's a doer, and she's devoted to the cause of helping women who are at risk, particularly at the hands of abusive men—and particularly in relationships, family settings, and the workplace. So many women have no idea of how to help themselves, and she's a bull-dog—she does it for them at first, then she takes them by the hand and shows them. She's an advocate and a teacher and a coach and a best friend, all in one." Worly paused as the coffees arrived and Winnie took their lunch order. Worly and Missy ordered Cobb salads. Dora ordered a chef's salad, claiming she would never order anything named Cobb, given her experience with the Cobb brothers.

Dora and Missy waited after Winnie had gone. Worly paused, her hands against the edge of the table, as though preparing to push it away.

"Then Shelly came," she continued. "Shelly was—ooh, how do I describe Shelly?" She looked at the ceiling, thinking. "Shelly was effusive, friendly, welcoming, joyful. She really was wonderful."

"Was Lillian jealous?" Missy asked.

"Probably"—Worly nodded—"but it was more than that. Shelly was all about helping women—keeping women safe, and at first, she and Lillian were best friends, and everything was"—Worly narrowed her eyes and tilted her head to either side—"more or less okay."

Realization dawned on Missy's face. "But she didn't consider Shelly a woman."

Worly nodded and pointed at Missy. "Well, biologically, she did. She accepted that part. Like most of us, she figured it wasn't her business. But in terms of her and the organization's purpose..." Celia cocked her head. "I think that was different. You have to understand what Lillian is about. Men take advantage of women. They use physical strength and positions of authority in families and jobs and all over society to put women down and keep them there."

"Oh, we get that," Missy said. The two women waited.

"But Shelly knew a lot of trans women and some non-binary people who also felt unsafe or were abused and had traumatic backstories. So she started bringing them in, and the ambiance of W.A.R. changed. The trans women—there were a few men, too, but mostly women—began to dominate the culture of the place, perhaps because their traumas were multileveled, or maybe because Shelly knew so many of them. Lillian lost control of the lifeline she had there, and she blamed Shelly."

"Have you ever heard of a man named Damian Wurtz?" Dora asked.

While Worly was considering the question, Missy reached into her pants pocket and drew out a piece of paper that featured the mug shot of a man with copper-colored hair, small blue eyes, a mustache and goatee, and some sort of green tribal tattoo on the lower left side of his neck. "Have you ever seen this man?"

Worly studied the picture, then shook her head. "I don't think so, and the name you mentioned doesn't ring a bell."

"Well," Dora said, her expression fixed on Worly, "if you hear any mention of him or see him, please reach out to us."

Worly's eyes went wide and flickered between the two investigators. "He's a murderer? Has he been at the center?"

Dora's tone was reassuring, yet focused. "Just be sure and let us know if there's evidence of him being around."

• • •

"So what do you think?" Missy asked as soon as they were back in Dora's car.

"I get that Lillian might be a bit possessive about Women at Risk. But killing people?" Dora shook her head. "I don't see that."

"Do you think Celia Worly's trying to distract attention from herself?" Missy asked.

"Could be. She's a hard person to read."

Missy agreed. "She's inscrutable."

"Good word," Dora said. "But it's still hard for me to get past the idea that Lorne Berger killed his sister for the inheritance, and Lee Travers somehow got in the way." She could see that Missy was convinced, her expression confidently fixed. "Especially after what Vanessa told us."

"It's what makes the most sense," Missy asserted.

"But let's talk to Lillian." Dora glanced at Missy to see her reaction and saw that she was willing. "I'd like to get a sense of her—not so much what she might specifically say, but, you know—a feel, once we bring some things up."

• • •

Dora parked the car a half block from the Women at Risk office. They approached the building together; Missy rang the buzzer next to the door to the street and waited. She rang again. Waited. Eventually a tall man with a long, frazzled gray beard exited the building, and Dora caught the door before it closed. She held it for Missy, and they climbed the narrow stairs to the landing outside the office. Dora knocked and peered through the blinds to the other side of the glass. There was no movement, and no one came to answer the door. She glanced at Missy, her eyebrows arched. She mouthed the word *Computer.*

"Aw, jeez—don't," Missy warned.

"Okay then," Dora responded, taking out an expired credit card and slipping it between the latch and the doorframe. Fortunately, the door was not dead bolted.

"Great," Missy whispered. "Now we're breaking and entering."

They entered the office, and Missy went directly to Lillian's desk and dipped a finger in a two-thirds-filled cup of coffee there.

"Still warm," she said. Then she moved to Lillian's computer, which displayed a multicolored screensaver. Missy moved the mouse. "Whoa —look at this!"

Dora had been looking over Missy's shoulder. On the screen was the word *HELP!*

Missy looked at Dora, who was already racing for the exit. "Wurtz took her." She saw Missy's baffled look.

"Got to be. Unless it was Lorne."

Missy's face lit up as they hurried to the car. "Know why it wasn't Lorne? The weapon. That suave guy—if he would kill anyone, he wouldn't use an automatic weapon. He'd use a handgun—probably something expensive."

Dora pressed her lips together. "You never know. If someone's a murderer, they might do anything. But I'm with you. Call it women's intuition or an educated investigator's guess. It was Wurtz!" They got into the turbo and roared away.

Chapter 23

"You're going to get pulled over," Missy mewed as they raced toward the parkways.

"I'm keeping an eye out," Dora replied, "and anyway, I'm not going that fast." Dora's attention was drawn to the right side of the car. "Look at that!" She pointed at a woman in her thirties who was looking at her phone while rocketing between lanes. "Long Island at its best." She sped up. "Anyway, Wurtz has to watch for cops too. I'll crank it when I can." As she said this, they entered a straightaway where there was no shoulder, and she stomped on the gas. The turbo took off.

"He won't outrun us with that truck," Dora promised.

Missy noticed the light in Dora's eyes and was at once terrified and excited. How many forms of insanity had she invited into her life?

While one part of her mind was in full flight, another continued to analyze and compute. "The fact that both victims knew Lillian would explain why they didn't run. She and Wurtz were probably in his truck together, knew where the victims would be, based on simple surveillance—"

"And," Dora turned toward Missy, "the fact that they were coming from Lillian's classroom."

"She probably got out of the truck and called to them, which put them at relative ease."

Dora was imagining the scenario. "Then Wurtz jumped out with the weapon."

"Hoo. Whoa!" Missy was veering back into anxiety. She looked out the window at the vegetation flashing by.

Dora was concentrating on both her driving and the narrative of the murders. "Then he kills them, tosses the weapon back into the vehicle, maybe wraps the victims in something—tarp, Trask said—to keep the blood from getting all over the truck, and tosses them into the back."

"What I want to know," Missy said, "is why no one saw this."

"Well, someone saw it when they transferred Lee to the beach."

"Right," Missy agreed, her mind once again moving at least as fast as the turbo, but in the opposite direction. "Where are we going?"

"So if Wurtz has gone off the rails and grabbed Lillian, he's going to the only place he feels comfortable."

"Ohhh," Missy moaned. "He lives in those computer games I found online and, you know, I'm not sure he deals with the real world."

Dora nodded, understanding. "The computer games *are* his real world, and the only place he knows, that's his turf—besides a game—is where he lives. That's where he's going."

They were traveling north on the Meadowbrook Parkway. Dora took the left lane toward the Southern State west.

"You don't think he went all the way up and took the Northern State?" Missy asked.

"To the degree I might understand this guy's thinking, I would think he'd want to always be getting to whatever the next road's going to be, as quick as possible." She glanced at Missy for confirmation.

Missy blinked a few times. "I guess that makes sense."

Dora nodded. "Same thing with the Throgs Neck Bridge. If I was in a hurry, I'd take the first bridge rather than wait for the Whitestone."

"But the Whitestone might have less traffic."

"It might, but he wouldn't know. He's not from around here."

"But he came down here at least a few times—to scope out his targets and to kill them."

"You're right," Dora admitted. "But there's one thing you're forgetting."

"And that is?"

Dora grinned. "I'm driving. So this is how we're going."

"Okay then."

They headed west on the Southern State, then took the Cross Island Parkway north toward the Throgs Neck Bridge, which would take them into the Bronx, then upstate.

"Taking the Hutch?" Missy asked, meaning the Hutchinson Parkway.

"Taking the Hutch," Dora confirmed.

"What about—?"

"There he is!" Dora spotted the Ford truck rounding a bend in the winding highway and sped up, until their turbocharged vehicle caught up and passed the black truck, which was in the right-hand lane. "Not him," Dora said. "Guess there's a lot of black Ford F-150s. This guy's bald, no beard and the truck's got different plates." Dora had already eased up on the gas.

Missy had relaxed, then sprang forward again.

"I think it's him! The neck tattoo. He cut his hair and shaved—and changed plates!"

Dora sped up. "You're right! Good job, Miss!" As she spoke, the bald man in the truck turned, saw the two women gawking and with a determined scowl, turned back to the road as the truck leaped ahead, then veered into the left lane, then veered right again to pass a slower car in the left. He did this several times so that in the space of perhaps three seconds, the truck was now three slower cars ahead of them.

• • •

Lillian was crouched on the right side of the floor in the front of the truck. She had been trying to talk to Wurtz, but he was ignoring her. He gripped the wheel with his left hand and a handgun in his right. She'd seen the automatic rifle on the floor in the back of the cab when he'd pushed her across the front seat.

"You don't need to do this! Just let me go! I won't say anything."

Silence.

"What do you have to gain by taking me?"

Silence.

She decided to change tactics. "We're on the same side here. Damian, I'm your friend."

Silence.

She tried desperately to soften her tone, but it was outside her wheelhouse. "Haven't I always paid you on time and the right amounts?"

Silence.

"I can pay you more. I know what! Let's go back to my bank—we can stop at my office, where I can get my checkbook. An ATM won't allow us to ... how much more would you like?"

"Shut up!" He waved the gun.

Her voice went up in pitch. She was growing agitated, hysterical. "The cops will be after both of us, so why don't we work together? Hey"—she tried to laugh, but only managed a weak gasp—"two heads are better than one."

That drew a grin from him and a barked laugh. She preferred the silence.

Finally he spoke. "You think I'm stupid, don't you?"

"No! No, I—"

"Shut the fuck up! I'm not some redneck, whatever you might think, and whatever you and your women"—he spat the word—"might think of men. You're the prejudiced one! You're the one with the problem." He waved the gun again, and Lillian cringed, petrified.

"I'll tell you what," Wurtz said. "Here's the deal. I live in a universe of technology beyond anything you could even think of. I've had people watching your communications, your office, your technology, and your assistant—people I don't even know! And that assistant's been talking to the cops, or people who work for the cops, anyways. So I decided to take a step back and lie low, but to guarantee I'm safe, I needed to bring you along for the ride. After a few days, maybe I'll come back and get rid of some of these threats."

Damian Wurtz opened all the windows in the truck, gave a quick glance around, and fired his Glock 19 out the window and into the air. Then he whooped with joy and pounded the steering wheel with his free hand.

"I've got you…under my skin!" he sang, and he pounded the wheel, stepped on the gas, and grinned at Lillian, who remained cowering on the floor.

· · ·

Women at Risk had been so wonderful, such a godsend—for them and for her. She had searched her whole life, well into her thirties, for meaning, for purpose. Searched might not be the right word—reeled was more accurate. But she'd been one of the lucky ones—her trauma had given her purpose. More accurately, she'd created her own. After working for another practice while going to school at night, she'd hung out her own shingle, so to speak, and begun with clients handed to her by a consulting company who hired credentialed women as contractors for their clients.

And then she'd networked like hell to develop her own clientele, which was easy enough, since her clients came from small business networking groups and were typically—though not all—women who were treated badly in the workplace or at home…by men. From there, starting her own organization was a natural outflow of her practice. So many women really were at risk!

She had taken so much crap herself, and nearly all of it from men. She had thought her career would be working for a women's service organization, like Planned Parenthood or a crisis center.

Once she had Women at Risk up and running, and the 501(c)(3) was set up and she had time to breathe, she was thrilled. She was ecstatic. And for a while, it really was a dream come true!

But then, these people. She couldn't have cared less about them; she would have been willing to help the first few. But there were hordes! They pushed into her territory and just kept coming. She had carved out this wonderful oasis. She was helping all these women, and it felt terrific. The first one came, and she was willing to help. *You want to call yourself a woman? I don't care. It's fine. But then two. Then five. And this Shelly person—she's got a crowd of people who follow her around— and they all say the same thing.* Everybody loves Shelly! Ooh, Shelly this. Shelly that! *Well,* not everybody *loves Shelly. Someone* hates *Shelly. Someone's* going to kill *Shelly. Because it's really Shelly's fault. There are social workers, therapists, groups that serve people like Shelly. Go there! But you can't say that.* Oh, no. *You have to help people who come in the doors. And why? Because you're a non-fucking-profit and you have a board and God forbid something's not run right and the board gets wind of it.* Fucking boards. Killing Shelly was brilliant. Maybe she should kill the board! But everyone looked to Shelly for help.

And on that stupid, stupid night, as she was driving out of the empty parking lot after the awful nightmare of seeing Damian kill Shelly, after thinking she was done with this whole sordid mess, she thought she saw Lee Travers looking out the window in the storm door at the back of the building. She couldn't be sure and was encouraged because Lee came to group the next day, and she was briefly hopeful, but the look Lee gave her—that look of terror told the story.

Chapter 24

Dora heard a single sharp *pop* and thought she saw Damian's hand out the truck window with a gun, but she couldn't be sure. She was doing her best to replicate the truck's maneuvers, but she had to take care not to endanger other motorists, let alone Missy.

The Hutchinson Parkway is, as parkways go, extremely winding and, as they came around a bend and into a straightaway, the truck was nowhere to be seen.

Dora stepped on the gas, and the little turbo raced around the next several curves, but the truck had vanished.

"He got off," Dora said. "Pull up your maps app. We're going to double back and figure out what he did. He's not getting away so easily."

"I don't need to," Missy announced. "I *know* what he did." She was thrown to one side as Dora took an exit, then to the other side as Dora re-entered the parkway in the other direction.

"He took the Cross County to the Sprain," Missy continued. "My cousins used to live up this way. We've been driving here since I was a kid. I should have thought of it before. Sorry."

Dora nodded. "You're forgiven." She followed Missy's instructions. "Hopefully he figures he lost us and has slowed down."

"At least a bit," Missy agreed hopefully. She shuddered. "You're driving awfully fast."

"Well—" Dora declared, as though to say *Of course, that's what's necessary.*

"You like this!"

"Well, yeah!" Dora laughed, as though that were obvious. "I'm going to try to run him off the road at the exit to the Sprain."

"Oh, for God's sake," Missy muttered, then continued whispering quietly.

"What is that you're saying?" Dora's face was lit with curiosity.

But Missy continued. "May our parents, our teachers, mentors, and our friends—may all living beings across the world, including and especially myself, be well, happy, peaceful, and safe!"

"Ooh, is that a Buddhist prayer?" Dora wanted to know.

Missy's eyes were closed. She nodded. "May no harm come to them, or to me. May we have the necessary patience, courage, understanding, and determination to meet and overcome inevitable difficulties, problems, and failures in life."

"Crap," Dora yelled. "He didn't get off at the Sprain."

Missy's eyes flew open. "Then the Saw Mill. He's taking the Saw Mill!"

"Yup, babe. He is!" Dora saw and followed the truck around the exit ramp.

"What's he doing?" Missy cried. "He's getting off the highway entirely. Shit—he's going to kill someone!"

"Ohhh. Hopefully not us!" Dora was squinting in the dying light. "He's going into a park or something."

"There's a golf course here—that must be where he's going."

Dora slowed down. "Well, now that we know where he's going, we need to figure out how to get to him and keep him from killing Lillian."

"Aren't we going to capture him?"

Dora looked at Missy as though she were crazy. "Capture him? I don't want to capture him." She stopped her car just short of the golf course parking lot and slightly around a bend, then got out of the car.

"You coming?"

"No!"

"Miss. Come on. I need your help."

"I was afraid you might say that. What am I—bait?"

"Not exactly."

"Will I not exactly be dead in a few minutes?"

Dora chuckled. "You're so cute."

• • •

The black Ford truck drove into the parking lot, made a small circle, and parked close to a clubhouse. Dora didn't follow but kept the turbo around the bend, where she felt she had options. Of course, Wurtz could see her, or knew more or less where she was, anyway. She wanted to give herself the option of running through the woods, which were thin but provided some cover. She also wanted to see if he would bring the AR-15 with him, or just the handgun, which she was pretty sure was either a Glock 19 or a Glock 43. If she was running through the woods and he took individual shots, she stood a much better chance than if he was spraying bursts in her direction. The trees were not only thin in number and had thin trunks, but were filled out with leaves now, which was good. She assumed he would take Lillian and the handgun with him and leave the AR-15 locked in the cab. That way, he would be able to shoot at her while handling Lillian, who didn't look like much but was young, small, wiry and possibly quick on her feet.

The closer Dora got to the truck and the clubhouse, which was just off the parking lot, the fewer the trees. One didn't see many trees on golf courses; the light was better, the golf was better. Dora had never understood golf; it was one of the many things she and Missy agreed upon.

While she didn't know what the relationship between Damian Wurtz and Lillian Walsh was, if any, Dora had seen him waving the handgun around and had to assume for that reason and safety's sake that he had taken Lillian against her will.

The truck was moving again. He had driven to the far side of the parking lot and up onto what little shoulder there was. Now he was out of the truck—no automatic rifle, Dora noted—and jogging around to its other side.

She had to do something before he disappeared into the trees.

She gunned the turbo into the lot and skidded to a stop a half dozen yards from the truck. She parked the driver's side toward Wurtz so that if he fired, Missy would be protected by the body of their car. She hadn't really planned to use Missy as bait. She had already allowed her to be in harm's way once—and in a parking lot, to boot! She wasn't doing that again.

She rolled down her window. "Come on, Damian—let her go. You don't need her!"

The only answer was two quick shots from his handgun, one of which hit the turbo's front left quarter panel. She tried not to think of the expense. She saw a woman's head moving over the truck's bed and realized he had pulled Lillian out the door.

"Wurtz!" she shouted, and when Wurtz turned, Lillian wrenched free and ran into the woods at a two o'clock diagonal—indirectly across Dora's line of vision.

Wurtz started after her and fired off two quick shots, but as Dora had suspected, Lillian was fast and spurred to even greater speed by adrenaline and fear.

Wurtz hesitated, looking after Lillian then at Dora, then back at Lillian, unsure of whom to chase. Lillian was moving into the trees, apparently unhurt.

Dora saw an opening created by his looking at Lillian and by the big truck between them. She sprinted suddenly toward Wurtz, then dropped and rolled in the direction of the truck's cab, keeping as much truck as possible between them.

Behind her, a car door slammed and she heard footsteps.

Missy! *What is Missy doing?*

"Get back in the car," Dora ordered as Wurtz fired again. He was on the other side of the truck, using the side of its bed as a gun rest. Assuming he'd started with a full magazine, Wurtz was unlikely to run out of ammunition anytime soon. He had started with at least 15 shots, standard in the Glock 19. Dora knew he may have had a magazine that held 17, 19 or as many as 33 rounds.

She got up to run but dropped as he fired again.

She looked around and made her decision. When she started running again, she zigzagged, hoping he'd miss, then, as she approached the truck, she used its driver's side footstep to leap into the air, onto the roof of the cab, then took a one-footed leap from the cab further into the air, and landed on Wurtz's shoulders.

They tumbled to the ground, and Dora rolled a few feet him. He had dropped his Glock and was scrambling on his hands and knees for it.

Dora was on her feet. She kicked him in the face, but he'd turned his head and rolled backward, taking some of the momentum from the kick. He just managed to grab the gun but must have sensed she was too close for him to take the time to turn and fire, because he scrabbled off into the ivy ground cover toward the trees.

Somewhere beyond them, Lillian was running and, Dora realized, Missy was chasing her.

She said a quick internal prayer, trying to remember the one Missy had said. She'd already lost one love—she just couldn't lose another!

Wurtz was wearing what looked to be heavy desert boots, so she knew she could run faster than him, and she was gaining. Wurtz seemed to sense this, because he stopped suddenly and turned to fire.

They were in the outskirts of the trees and about to head deeper into the thicket, but before Wurtz could shoot or turn to run again, Dora leaped up several feet into the air next to a tree, then used her right foot to kick herself off the tree trunk, all of which took a fraction of a second and had the effect of vaulting Dora into the air, then suddenly changing direction using the tree.

And then she was on him. In an instant she had broken his wrist, taken the gun, and beaten him unconscious with it. Blood leaked from one of his ears; more blood oozed from a gash below his eye. His hand was twisted grotesquely in the wrong direction against his wrist.

She held the gun to his crotch and spoke out loud. "You reap what you sow, my friend." But then she imagined Missy's voice telling her to "exercise restraint for a change." *Shut up, Miss,* she thought, but considered their possible new living arrangement and, with a pang of guilt, she shook her head and shot Wurtz in the leg, which would keep him from going anywhere.

Still holding the gun, Dora ran in the direction she had heard Lillian and Missy heading. Noting bent branches and trampled ground cover, Dora fought through the underbrush until she came to a clearing that was a tee area—the golf course's first tee—and she was stunned by what she saw, and powerless to intervene. Lillian was about to launch herself, small, dark, wiry—enraged—at Missy.

Poor chubby, little intellectual librarian Missy. Dora's hand went involuntarily to her mouth.

But Missy did something so unexpected that Dora could only watch and remind herself to breathe. Missy—*her Missy!*—performed a near perfect, if slightly awkward, roundhouse kick to the back of Lillian's front knee, where the diminutive woman's weight was planted. Then, as Lillian started to stumble forward and tried to catch herself, Missy clipped the side of her jaw with an absolutely impressive right cross.

Right. On. The. Button.

Lillian went down—out cold.

And Dora started to laugh. By the time she got to her and wrapped Missy in her arms, holding her, the tears coming, Missy was embarrassed.

"Oh my God. I'm so violent. I'm everything I didn't want—" She began to shake.

"Shhh, Miss. You were wonderful. Perfect. You saved the day, babe."

Missy held her at arm's length. "Oh, come off it. You nailed the guy with the gun."

• • •

Dora and Missy were silent as they waited for the police to arrive. Dora was still filled with adrenaline and was decompressing. Missy was hugging herself and crying intermittently. Now and then she grasped Dora by the arm or laid her head on Dora's shoulder. Dora would comfort Missy later but would need to have her own trauma at least somewhat relieved before that.

Lillian could not stop talking.

First she protested her innocence. "Thank God you guys showed up. He was going to kill me. Oh, thank God!"

Dora's expression remained impassive. "We know you were behind this, so don't go there."

"How could you think such a thing? That lunatic—he had some kind of machine gun and—"

"Come on." Dora's annoyance with Lillian must have helped Missy pull herself together because she spoke up. "What was his motive? Why would he even be here? He's not from around here and has no connection to Shelly and Lee. Where's he from?"

"He's from upstate…" Lillian realized she had said too much and stopped talking for a moment. Missy smiled.

But soon, Lillian started talking again. She must have forgotten her *faux pas*. "That man's crazy. A misogynist! Hates women. Hates transgender women! Hates nonbinary people! He's a hateful man—a terrorist!"

Dora exchanged glances with Missy, then sent a scornful scowl toward Lillian. "You're confusing him … with you."

"No!" Lillian protested. "He was kidnapping me!"

Missy had had enough. She'd been standing next to Dora, who had pressed Lillian against a tree and twisted one of her arms up and behind her back.

"Cut the crap! I have your emails, screenshots of the money you paid him through that app. And I figured out how you stopped Shelly and Lee in their tracks by calling out to them from Wurtz's truck. That's why they stopped long enough for him to kill them."

"Well, there—you see! I didn't kill anybody."

"You were an accessory," Dora snarled. "Besides, that's for the police to sort out."

And Lillian started to moan softly, which rose into a wail as her ego and denial were punctured by the truth Missy had forced in front of her. The wail was long and rising and crescendoed, then began to fall, until she was sobbing pitifully. But neither Dora nor Missy had any room for pity for this woman.

She then began to speak; she was difficult to understand at first, she was crying so hard, but as she spoke, her cadence smoothed, and her speech became clearer.

"I lost jobs because of men. I had to work harder, do more for less, because of men. I've taken crap from men since fifth grade, when Jimmy Elton pinned me to the ground next to the gate at school and stuffed rocks down my shirt. And do you know what Jimmy Elton did when we were all grown up?"

Dora sighed. "I guess you're gonna tell us."

"Jimmy Elton raped me! That piece of shit told me he was going to take what he'd always wanted, and there wasn't a damned thing I could do about it. He said it was what I wanted too—but I had no say in the matter. That, that pig! What I wanted…what I wanted was to cut off his damned parts. He said he could do whatever he wanted right then and do you know what? He was right. That's just what he did."

She began to growl like an animal—like a wolf. "He ruined my life. I was fifteen years old, and I got pregnant. I was ruined, as far as my parents were concerned. I'm from an Irish Catholic family. Do you know what my father did?"

Dora looked curious. "He killed Jimmy Elton?"

"Ha! I wish. He sent me to Ireland—Poppintree, Ireland, which is north of Dublin and is where our people are from." Her speech took on a hint of a brogue when she mentioned Ireland.

Dora nodded and pursed her lips in distaste.

"And I had that baby there—the most beautiful creature I'd ever seen." She began crying again. "I had to give my beloved Laura up for adoption! And, who took her from me? Men! So I came back, and I made damned lemonade. I made a safe space where there were no men. No men! I made what I wished I'd had—a place to go, where they'd have taken care of me—where they'd have loved me. A place without men. But then—" She stopped crying. A river of snot was sliding down the space between her nose and her lips and had slipped to her chin and begun to drip down the front of her shirt. She caught her breath.

"But then, the men came. Not regular men, but men who could weasel their way into Women at Risk because they were pretending to *be* women at risk."

"But why kill anyone, Lillian?" Dora asked. "Why would you kill anybody when you were helping so many people? I don't get it. It doesn't make sense!"

"She felt threatened," Missy muttered.

Lillian's face contorted with rage; she struggled against Dora's hold, but Dora tightened her grip until Lillian cried out in pain.

"That place was mine!" She snarled. "Women at Risk was mine! No men—no men! NO MEN!"

Missy stood next to Lillian so that the enraged woman could not avoid looking into Missy's face, given the way Dora had her locked up. "Shelly and Lee *were* women, Lillian," Missy said, "and they needed your help! Let me tell you something, lady. You don't like misogynists—you're just as bad. Your purpose was to help women, but you not only let them down, you murdered two."

"And I'll tell you why," Lillian said. "Because fuck them!" She spat the words out. "Fuck them! I wouldn't let them ruin Women at Risk—and yeah, I'm sorry I got caught, but I'd do the same damned thing again. Every day I would!"

"You won't get that chance," Dora murmured as the sound of sirens and arriving police cars filled the golf course parking lot.

Epilogue

At the police station, they saw Mallard and Ganderson seated at their desks with a woman they later learned was Paula Ricci, Lorne's sister, who was indeed entitled to a half share of the family fortune, with the rest going to Lorne.

Vanessa declined to press charges, so Lorne was free to go and begin to enjoy his new fortune, but not before Rudy offered him a few choice words of warning.

Over the next two weeks, during which time the pair took a well deserved vacation, Dora began to move herself and her possessions, including her dog, Freedom, to Missy's apartment, which was the larger of their two living spaces.

On the afternoon they were finished, they stopped at the office of Geller Investigations to say hello. They were greeted by Thelma, with her usual effervescence.

"Well, if it isn't Nicky and Nora Charles," the office manager intoned.

"She's saying we're thin," Missy commented, alerting Thelma to the fact that she knew that the two investigators she was referencing were the main characters in Dashiell Hammett's *The Thin Man*.

"Congratulations, ladies!" Adam had come out from the back of the office, where he had no doubt been watching reruns of *The Odd Couple* on his iPad.

"Hey!" Dora cried, bumping elbows with their boss.

Missy grinned and bumped fists with Adam. "How's your health?"

Adam gave a wan smirk. "Holding up. I start radiation in about ten days. Brachytherapy—implants of radioactive seeds the size of grains of rice."

"When do they take them out?" Dora asked.

"Never."

"Just water him, put him in the sunlight and watch him grow," Thelma muttered.

"So are you going to cut back on your workload?" Dora wondered.

"Hah!" Thelma laughed.

"Quite the contrary," Adam corrected. "I want to do *more*, by which I mean I want to be in it. So I have a proposition for you."

Thelma shot him a look. "Thought you have to go easy on the sex when you have prostate cancer."

Adam rolled his eyes. "For one thing," he continued, "I'm not sure I'm going to need an office manager, going forward."

Thelma's eyebrows went up. Adam waved a finger at her.

Dora barked a laugh.

"I know you're not serious," Thelma retorted. "Place'd go down the tubes in no time. Wouldn't last a month without me."

"I want to offer you two women a partnership—with you sharing half, with mine being the other half." He looked at Dora and Missy with a half smile. "And we'd split the caseload. I'd like to do some real detective work—on real criminal cases. And you'd get some of the divorces and disability cheats."

"Um, that sounds fantastic," Dora said, exchanging a glance with Missy, "but can we take a day or two to discuss it before we let you know? We sort of have a lot to get used to as it is."

"She's right," Missy agreed.

"Of course! I didn't mean to put you on the spot." Adam beamed at them both. "I also want you to know how grateful I am that you're safe. You're a couple of tough cookies."

"Ooh, cookies," Missy said softly. "We were just about to go out for dinner. Why don't you come?"

"Can't, but don't let me stop you." Adam stood to one side so Dora and Missy had a clear path to the door.

They celebrated that night with dinner at The Elegant Lagoon, followed by their first night together at their new, shared apartment.

"I was afraid you wouldn't want to move in with me," Dora said, as she enjoyed a beer.

"Why would you think such a thing?" Missy wanted to know.

"Because bring private investigators is dangerous."

"I know." Missy's eyes widened, and Dora saw a glint in them. "I've experienced the danger. I've even *caused* some of it!"

"Also because my personality is such a weird mixture of sensitivity and violence. How would you deal with that ongoing?" she asked cautiously.

Missy was smiling now. "I wouldn't change it. I love you—including all your reactions and feelings and behaviors and inclinations and warts—they're all part of your beauty to me."

Dora's lips were pressed tight; her eyes were tearing.

"I've figured out the secret to life," Missy said softly. "It's the answer to just about everything."

This took Dora by surprise. "What?"

Missy took her hand and kissed it. "Love."

THE END

Charlie Bernelli III, better known as C3, was with his wife, the journalist Sarah Turner, and their young daughter Olivia. They were enjoying a musical, theatrical event put on by young people who were special in the way that Olivia was special.

They were having a wonderful time. As the voices of the cast and chorus sang the penultimate line of the final song and took a breath to sing the song's last line, a shrill scream filled the brief silence. In the pandemonium that followed, C3 and Sarah cradled their daughter between them and rushed from the playhouse where the event was being held.

It was only later that they learned that the understudy for one of the leads and the assistant director, Julian Lockhart, himself a man with special needs, had been murdered.

One week later, Mr. Lockhart's parents, Maverick and Ruby, hired Geller Investigations to look into the death of their son, but what Dora and Missy were to uncover was so much more than a single isolated murder. *How would the pair survive an investigation that was to prove more challenging and dangerous than any they'd ever known?*

Look for Book 5 in David E. Feldman's

Dora Ellison Mystery Series: A Special Storm.

Dear Reader: Thanks so much for reading A Biological Storm.
I hope you will join my mailing list to learn more about my next books at:
https://www.davidefeldman.com/books.shtml

If you enjoyed this book, I would be grateful if you would post a review online.

See you again soon!

-DF